I0630222

SEVEN MIRRORS

Damon

M. Bradley

Copyright © 2015 M. Bradley
All rights reserved.

ISBN: 0692473122

ISBN 13: 9780692473122

TABLE OF CONTENTS:

Prologue	v
Chapter One: Dragged	1
D	1
A	4
M	5
O	7
N	11
Chapter Two: Downward Spiral	14
D	14
A	16
M	24
O	27
N	28
Chapter Three: Obsessions	32
D	32
A	37
M	39
O	44
N	46
Chapter Four: Unleashed	48
D	48
A	49
MO	52
N	54
Chapter Five: Fallen	58
D	58
A	61
MO	64
N	67

Chapter Six: Protocol Breach	70
D	70
A	76
M	79
O	81
N	84
Chapter Seven: Broken Code	88
D	88
A	90
M	93
O	94
N	99
Chapter Eight: DAMON	101
D	101
A	103
M	104
O	106
N	108
Epilogue	113

PROLOGUE

The light seemed to hang in the air, as still and timeless as the books upon the shelf. Row after row, stacked against one another and piled to the sides, old cloth covers with worn edges and faded lettering painted her favorite mosaic.

Amanda Pace was not one of those people who claimed to love the smell of an old book. In a very practical way, she thought most old items smelled like the same combination of dust and mildew, sprinkled with a hint of rodent. There was no love of raising yellowed pages to her face and breathing in the exotic and yet predictable smell. For Amanda, the love went deeper than that. To her, age was a gift not everything would be enjoyed. Those few things that could stand the test of time and last for generations drew a certain level of respect that she simply couldn't ignore.

She felt admiration for the items that had lived beyond their expected time.

She felt affection for the items that by quality or chance had not yet made it to the rubbish pile.

She felt a special pity for the brilliant works of art and literature which sat, rotting upon some forgotten ledge, unused and unloved. It was the reason most weekends involved a trip to the antique shops and thrift stores in her town. Amanda's finger would drag over the spines and she would feel like an emperor with the power to save the condemned from the pit of lions. While most would fade, rot, and someday disintegrate in some landfill, a select few could again be a useful book, spending the rest of its days upon the shelf of someone who cared.

It was a tad romantic of her, but she was so rarely romantic in other ways that it didn't seem that strange.

Amanda never took home a book she didn't intend to read; just as she never bought a painting she didn't intend to hang. Books were written to be read, and she had been cover to cover with every piece in her home. Today, with a cool coffee weighing down one hand, she would select the next batch of refugee books and thus keep them alive for a little longer.

She read the covers silently, trying to find the ones that seemed to offer the most. Amanda rarely read non-fictions, finding it boring and overly opinionated. She figured that each biography was no more than a doctored version of history; a carefully decorated telling of real events, crafted to make you believe one set of truths over another. What was fair? What was real? What was accurate? She preferred fiction, where at least she knew the writer was lying to her.

Amanda's finger slipped over the bindings and the names of the books blurred together like a mumbling in her head. Nothing reached her.

The Sacred Sacrifice. Sounded a little heavy for how she was feeling.

You Are Lost...depressing.

One Shot at Love.... even more depressing.

Love and Hate. She was sure that one would end up being cheesy.

The Spirits in the Seven Mirrors... the name was too long, and the title was vague but then she wondered; are there spirits in each mirror? How many? Why are there ghosts in the mirrors? Is this horror? Or suspense? Or fantasy? Could spirits be in a mirror? Why trap spirits in something so frail? What is this book?

Amanda hooked the top of the volume with a curved finger and plucked it away from the others on the shelf. The book felt too heavy, but dangerously frail. It was as though the smallest misstep would lead to hundreds of pages piled on the floor, yet there was so much the author wanted to say all in one edition.

She carefully pulled open the front cover, listening to the crackling of the spine and gentle popping of the pages while she drew a long and nervous breath. There was no summary. There was no information page. There was the name of a printing house in Boston, and it was dated 1822.

Amanda reeled at the date. In her hand was the oldest book she had ever found, and it was massive. Most old books were tiny compared to today's novels, with the big ones only coming into fashion in the 1900s. How did this one ever get printed?

Everything about the book captured Amanda's attention. She gingerly flipped through the pages until she stumbled upon an outline drawing of a man in a black suit with a long jacket, holding a rectangular panel and staring into it with a frightfully intense look upon his face. The cover of the panel bore the image of a screaming expression, and some dark substance seemed to be dripping from one corner in small droplets. Amanda pressed the book closed again and looked over the simple gold-leaf lettering on the cover.

She had to have this book.

The woman at the register did not seem the least impressed as Amanda strained to hide the excitement she felt over the rarity of her find. She placed the book on the counter, along with a pair of more recent works, and fought to keep her expression neutral. Of course the cashier saw hundreds of dusty old books every day, and the thrift shop was full of throwaway items, none of which were probably that interesting to the middle-aged woman in the blue apron. Everything in here would most likely seem like piles of unwanted items to those who worked there. In fact, Amanda was willing to assume most of the inventory came from homes of the deceased, especially the older items. So, in that sense, the cashier worked at the equivalent of a funeral home "lost and found".

"Is everything all right, honey?"

The dour voice of the cashier drew Amanda out of her thoughts, and she realized she was laughing. "I'm good," she assured the woman behind the register.

"A lot of reading," the woman continued, eyeing the books suspiciously. She snagged up The Spirits in The Seven Mirrors roughly and Amanda gasped.

"Careful," she instructed, then regretted the command in her tone. Smiling apologetically, Amanda explained, "That's just a really old book, and I don't want it to fall apart quite yet."

The woman in the apron knit her brow at Amanda and made an exaggeration of placing the book in its own sack and placing it away from the other items. A faint smile lurked under her nose, during the whole process.

"Thank you," Amanda said, trying to salvage the moment.

The cashier rolled her eyes and Amanda paid as quickly as she could. Taking her things, she strolled out the front doors at a quick pace, cradling her new books like a mother leaving the hospital with her first born. She slipped into the driver seat of her four-door Celica – another thing in her life that had seen far too many years, and gently pulled the door closed behind her. Peeling away the thin plastic until the cover was exposed; Amanda studied her find with all the excitement of a successful treasure hunter. The book looked back up at her with promises of long nights and interesting tales.

The questions kept loitering in her mind. What were the spirits? What were the mirrors? The black goo in the picture and the man in the long coat. Who were they? What was he doing to the panel? Was that the glass? Everything about this book was a mystery.

"The grey dove flew away with the letter. I would say she is totally hooked," said the cashier in the apron, and she put back the speaker of the ancient, black, rotary dial telephone, which looked like an item for sale in the thrift shop. Few people would have thought it is actually working. She smiled and went back to the cash machine, after seeing Amanda's car pulling away.

1

DRAGGED

"**N**o way, man."

Aaron tipped his head back and let out a long, disappointing moan.

"Make all the noise you want," Detrick replied in an offended tone. "Your idea is stupid, and there is no way I'm in."

The two exchanged looks, one a pleading grimace and the other obstinate and immobile.

Aaron sighed and popped the tip of his pinkie in his mouth. "So there is no convincing you?" he asked around his fingernail.

Around them, the restaurant buzzed and clattered its continual song. Servers strode past, laden with too much food while the kitchen clinked and hissed. The patrons freely laughed and talked and ate as though their tables were islands of privacy and no one was listening in. Aaron carried on in a similar fashion, but his companion was more reserved.

"You want me to dress in drag," Detrick began.

"Not in drag," Aaron interrupted. "I just want you to pose as a homosexual for one night."

The look on Detrick's face could have made a homicide detective think carefully before speaking again.

Unfortunately, Aaron was not a homicide detective.

"You go in, flirt with the bartender, and take a quick look around," he explained. "That's it. You're gay for like ten minutes, tops."

"Do you have any idea how offensive you sound?" Detrick questioned. "I mean, you're talking as though I am dressing up as a fireman or a policeman."

"Don't be ridiculous," Aaron spat loudly. "A cop would gather too much attention. I need you to blend in."

"By acting gay?"

"It's a gay bar!" he explained.

The space around them went quiet after the announcement, but Aaron didn't seem to notice.

"She keeps going in there and says she's only hanging out with her friends, but why at a gay bar?" Aaron huffed. "I mean really. What's up with that?"

"Maybe she just doesn't enjoy being hit on constantly," Detrick suggested quietly.

Aaron ruffled his own hair, the dirty golden strands bouncing happily under his sweeping fingers, and growled in his throat. "She's cheating on me, man," he said. "I know it. I know she is."

"You know no such thing," Detrick contended. "You've always been a jealous guy, though."

"A woman that hot does not just hang around though, man," Detrick declared. "She's going to get offers."

"So be happy she's drinking with friends in a place where that is least likely to happen." Detrick sipped his coffee and smiled at his friend. "Because I am not spying on her for you," he added.

"Asshole," Aaron grumbled, though they both knew the word had no teeth.

"I had that dream again," Detrick shared, desperate to change the topic.

His companion gave a tired laugh and rolled his eyes. "Again?" he asked. Both of them knew Aaron wasn't commenting on the frequency of the dream as much as the regularity of this conversation.

"It never changes, man," Detrick pressed like a man who can no longer keep a secret. "Every time I have it, it's the same thing."

"The creepy guy scratching his way out of your colon," Aaron mumbled.

"He's fighting his way out of me," Detrick shot back in an irritated voice.

"You said from your bowels," Aaron reminded his friend.

"As in the deepest part of me," Detrick clarified.

"And yet I've only ever heard bowels referred to as the poop chamber," Aaron said in a smug tone. "Thus," he said with a wave of his hand, "you have monsters in your colon."

"This time it was different, though," Detrick persisted.

"When you think about it," Aaron inserted, "when two people kiss on the mouth they're really just connecting anuses."

"Aaron!" Detrick barked. "Focus."

"You want me to listen to this but you're unwilling to listen to my ideas?"

"Your ideas include me making a mockery of the gay community for your own selfish concerns."

"She's meeting dudes at the gay bar!" Aaron declared. "I know it."

"I think the man inside me was real," Detrick decided.

"Oh for the love of..." Aaron groaned.

"And I don't think he wants out anymore."

<u>A</u>

Amanda closed her car door and walked up to her townhouse home. She undid the lock and quickly slipped inside. The air in the room was lightly scented from a clear glass bowl of potpourri on the short table by the door. Amanda lifted the lid, which was decorated with a number of curved cutouts in a spiraling pattern, and set it on the table. She flapped her hand over the bowl, an action she had watched her mother perform a thousand times, and breathed in the air spiced with rose, citrus, and cinnamon.

The room was dim with the heavy curtains over the front windows, but the low light made Amanda feel peaceful and relaxed. Outside, the world was loud and busy, constantly pushing a person to race from one spot to the next. Amanda soldiered through her days with a plastered smile and an active thought life, keeping mostly to herself and avoiding any personal contact. It wasn't that she didn't like people in general. There were plenty of examples all around her of men and women with kind hearts and generous spirits.

Though she probably trusted the latter least of all.

There was nothing wrong with people, but she had immense trouble understanding why someone would be good to her in particular. Amanda questioned every deed and every statement with a passionate scrutiny. "There is always another shoe about to drop," she liked to say. "There is always a hidden motive."

That's why she loved books so much. Never had they betrayed her. Never had they done her wrong. Never had they pretended to love her and then left her with nothing. Books could be disappointing, but they weren't malicious; they never asked her for anything.

They were the perfect companions.

And each new book was like a new love. Amanda would wrap herself in a story with all the energy of a young woman in a new relationship. She would miss meals, lose sleep, and daydream about a story right up to the last line. All of the energy she had would go into the book, and once finished she would set it upon her shelf as a reminder of everything they had been through. To some, it would have seemed a tad extreme, but to Amanda it only made sense. She was going to spend a portion of her life with this work – hours that she would never again have – and it was only fitting in her mind to honor that time.

These were the thoughts running through Amanda's head as she gently laid the thrift shop bag upon her two-chair dining table. She lifted the plastic slowly and lovingly, taking care to remove the book as though she were handling a museum piece. The book nestled comfortably in her hand and she stood there, locked in space for a moment as she admired the aged cover.

She didn't bother with tea.

She didn't bother with wine.

Amanda glided to her short sofa and wedged herself in one corner. The book rested upon her lap, and Amanda took a deep breath before cracking it open.

<u>M</u>

Frankly, it was a comical sight. The man hunched over the paper was far too big for the little antique secretary desk and the chair he was occupying. The corners of the piece had been worn round from years of use, and its most recent owner didn't seem bothered by the shabbiness of its appearance. He himself was a study in presentation, with his large belly, rounded shoulders, and balding head encircled with fiery red hair and a long beard. The sleeves of tattoos added to the mixture, and the slippers on his feet made him seem older than he really was.

"Is this going to hurt?"

The tattoo artist looked up from his transfer paper and rolled his eyes. "Nope," he said sarcastically.

"It is, isn't it?" the client said.

He spun in his chair and smiled at the young lady nervously wringing her hands. "Yes," he said flatly. "It is going to feel like a cat scratching a sunburn, or a million little bites from a million tiny little tigers, or countless pinches from itty-bitty little angry fingers."

"Really?" the girl asked with a worried expression.

"Yup," the artist said, turning back to his table. "Or you'll hardly feel it at all. Everybody's different... uh..." He leaned to read the name on the tattoo order.

"Michaela," she offered.

"Sure," he said indifferently. "Michaela. No one's experience is the same. Now," he said, holding up the sketch of the tattoo, "what do you think?" The image was a tribal symbol with long hooks spread out at the bottom and peaking at the top, like a pyramid made of large thorns. "I've changed a little here on the..."

"No," the girl replied in a firm voice. "It has to be just like what I drew."

"You got it," the artists said, wadding his rendition and dropping it in the trash, clearly offended. "It's your chest, but it's not going to fit the way you think it will."

Michaela took a deep breath and steadied herself. She didn't know why this was so important to her, but she had secretly always wanted a tattoo, and she had it in her mind that this was the perfect one for her. "I'm sorry," she said softly, recognizing that the man scarring her for life was not the person she should be upsetting. "I am ready for it to look a little weird, but I just really want it to be exactly like I drew it."

"You know there was another kid who came in here this week with a picture of his own," the artist shared, pouring a cup of jet-black ink. "He was every bit as insistent as you on having his picture transferred exactly. Same kind of image too. You in some cult?"

Michaela laughed in short, shocked bursts of air. "No," she managed. "Definitely not."

"Funny," he said, plugging in the tattoo machine and making it sing.

"Is that the gun?" she asked, a little worried by the dentist office noise coming from the contraption.

"Nope," the artist said. "Guns kill people. This is a tattoo machine. It makes permanent art." He then fed her drawing into a small printer at the corner of his desk.

Michaela made a frustrated noise and shook her head. "So that's the thing though, right? That's the, uh…"

"The buzz buzz that will make the ouchy ouch?" the artist retorted. He picked up her drawing, now copied onto transfer paper, and held it up for her to see. The image was crudely drawn, like a child's art fair entry, and seemed lopsided. But like the ugliest dog at the shelter, Michaela looked upon the sketch with a deep and unexplainable sense of affection. "So are we doing this then?" he asked bluntly.

"Definitely," she said, leaning back in the tattoo chair.

The artist slid over and pressed the image over her cleavage with medical familiarity. He held up the mirror for her to check, and when Michaela gave the nod, the tattoo machine began to whir with a maddening consistency.

O

"Sir!" the receptionist called, bursting through the swinging doors that led into the examination hallway. Her tennis shoes squeaked and her voice cracked as she hurried to catch the young man. "You cannot just come back here. Sir!"

It was the emergency room's busiest time of the evening, and every member of the staff was buried on one room or another. A cleaning person watched the scene from down the hall before slipping nervously into a side room.

The man didn't seem to hear the receptionist. He dove into the first room he could find and tore aside a privacy curtain. "Doctor!" he screamed, terrifying the couple assigned to that room. The man in the bed twisted and pressed a bloodied pad to his forearm while the woman shrieked and recoiled. Unsatisfied that there were no physicians in the room, the young man turned back to the hall.

The receptionist reached him as he was exiting and tried to block him from going any further. The man shoved the receptionist and moved on to the next room.

"Eric!" the receptionist screamed into the empty hallway, praying that someone would hear. "Get security!"

"Doctor!" the young man screeched into the next room. He took a single step into the room before finding it empty. "No," he said, pitching forward and holding his stomach.

"Now hold it right there!" the receptionist barked, blocking the door. "You are…" The words caught in her throat as she looked over the young man.

Doubled over and turning purple, the man fell to the floor in a loud crash against the bedside table. His mouth was open and straining while his eyes were pressed so tightly that the receptionist feared he would burst a vessel. The young man turned on the floor and rolled to his face, kicking his legs and making sounds like long dry heaves.

"Doctor Troost!" the receptionist screamed. "Doctor! Eric! Anybody!"

The man on the floor hacked and spat until a black fluid stained his teeth and marred his chin. Dr. Troost pushed her way past the receptionist and laid a gloved hand upon the man.

"Sir?" she asked in a strong and steady voice.

Eric the nurse moved in beside Dr. Troost and looked over his arms and legs.

"Careful," Troost warned her nurse. "There's a fresh tattoo on the outside of his right forehand, and it looks as though it was damaged."

Eric gingerly inspected the sight and found a rough-drawn symbol with curves and loops, covered in blood and seeping ink.

"Hope he didn't pay much for that," Eric muttered, earning the reproving eye of his doctor. "Just sayin'."

"Sir?" Troost asked, moving herself to see the man's face more clearly. "Sir, can you hear me?"

"I need a doctor!" the man screamed into her face. "Help me!"

"I'm a doctor," she replied in a steady and practiced tone. "I am here to help you, but I need to know what is happening."

"I let it out!" the man cried.

"What's your name?" Eric asked, looking over the young man's chest and back.

"Orin," the man growled. "Help me," he panted, his eyes suddenly growing clear and filled with worry. "Help me. Please. I let it out."

"Let what out, Orin?" Troost asked.

"The thing inside me," Orin cried, tears working down his cheeks. "The thing inside me. It's coming. It's getting out. I let it out. Oh God! I let it out."

"Amphetamines?" Eric suggested, only this time the look from the doctor was worried.

"No other signs," she said quickly. "Long board!" the doctor ordered into the hall. "We need him in a bed," she told Eric who nodded his agreement. "Orin?" she asked, turning back to her patient. "Orin we need to move you to a bed so that I can help you, okay? We're going to slip a board under you and lift you onto a bed so that we... Holy shit. Twenty-one!"

Orin's body fell limp, unrolling into an ugly pile at the doctor's knees. Eric slapped a button beside the entrance to the room and a yellow light flickered in the hallway. Staff raced into the room, responding to the emergency call, but when they arrived the nurses found Troost and Eric, quickly backpedaling out the doorway, their faces white with shock.

"No!" the doctor ordered, holding out her arm to prevent anyone from entering the room. Tennis shoes squeaked to a halt as the staff looked first with nervous curiosity at Troost and Eric before leaning to look inside the examination room.

"Doctor Troost?" one of the nurses asked, watching the sweat pour off the physician. Her eyes were wide, with huge black pupils, and her mouth was hanging open. The shaken appearance of the seasoned and normally controlled ER doctor made the nurse all the more worried for what she was hiding in the room.

"Stand aside," barked a commanding voice from behind the group. Everyone except for Eric and Dr. Troost looked to find Dr. Blankenship threading his way through the growing crowd. He had the air of a proven military general and the confidence of a lion. He pushed staff aside by their shoulders, parting the group as though they were mere children. Everyone folded before him until his hand landed on Dr. Troost.

Troost grabbed Blankenship's wrist with one hand and placed the other upon his chest. "No," she ordered.

"Dr. Troost," Blankenship said with as little respect of the title as he could manage. "You called for emergency assistance." He yanked his wrist free and looked down on her with competitive distrust.

"Call the police," she demanded.

"What?" Blankenship shot back. "Why? What's going on in there?" He tried to move past her but Troost held her ground.

"You can't go in there," she insisted. "I don't know what is wrong with him but he is dangerous, and no one…"

"If there is a sick man in that room it is our job to…"

"No one goes in that room, dammit!" Troost snapped violently. The nurses flinched and took a step back, but Blankenship held his ground. "Anyone who goes in that room before the police arrive is fired," she declared loudly, staring into Blankenship's suspicious eyes.

"You don't give orders to me," Blankenship growled. "I will not abandon a man if there is something I can do about it." Troost tried to hold him back but Blankenship overpowered her, brushing his fellow doctor to one side and stepping into the doorway. That was as far as he made it before Blankenship stomped to a halt. Standing in the middle of the room, taking in the view of the reflection of his well-built upper body, bulging with muscles, in the mirror, raising a bloodstained hand was Orin, his new tattoo radiating a soft purple light.

N

Nicolette grabbed a tuft of her own hair and ground her teeth. She had trusted Carrie with more than she had ever shared with anyone else, and this was the result? The two had been arguing for the last half-hour over the most unimportant details, and Nicolette had endured just about as much as she could manage.

"It's just that the dreams don't seem as critical to me as they do to you that's all," Carrie said in a voice that sounded more patient than she felt. "You keep talking about this internal struggle and this force wanting to get out..."

"It doesn't want out." Nicolette growled. "It wants control."

"Of you?" Carrie asked in a disbelieving tone.

Her sister stared back with a cold frustration.

"Don't glare at me," Carrie warned. "You wanted to talk about your dream. You wanted my opinion. Now you're going to have a fit because my view is different from yours? Really?"

Nicolette kept her lips pressed tightly closed.

"I think, little sister," Carrie sang in the same tone their mother used to take in situations such as this, "that you should pay more attention to what happens to you when you are awake. How's work? How's your love life?"

"You would rather talk about the last time I got laid?" she grumbled in return. "Just... Just leave, then."

Carrie stood and looked around. The two had been sitting in Nicolette's small living room since Carrie had arrived, and she was ready for a change of venue. The apartment couldn't be described as spacious in any sense of the term, but Nicolette had done her best to expand the space with mirrors and small furniture pieces. The windows to the rear looked out over the bay, and the view from there on the fifth floor was nothing to scoff at. If it wasn't for the view, the apartment may never have held any appeal.

Carrie stretched and headed to the kitchen. "Need a drink?"

Nicolette brought her knees to her chest and twisted into a ball on the loveseat.

"Water?" Carrie pressed. When her sister did not reply, she poured a glass from the tap before pouring a mug of water for herself. While her mug was heating in the microwave, Carrie set her sister's glass on the coffee table.

Nicolette held her pose.

The timer beeped and Carrie disappeared for a moment. She re-emerged with a hot cup of tea and resumed her place beside her sister. Nicolette broke her position only long enough to steal the tea from her sister's offended hand.

"Thanks," Nicolette muttered.

"It wasn't for you," Carrie assured her.

"All the same."

Carrie picked up the untouched glass of water and took a sip. Her eyes drifted to the little sister's nervous frame and a new sense of concern bubbled up her chest. "You're really freaked out by all this?"

Nicolette looked to her sister out of the corner of her eye, her lips again pressed into a hard line.

"What is it?" Carrie asked, her words thick with concern.

"It's not a dream," Nicolette said in a small voice.

Carrie leaned in close but kept her mouth silent.

Nicolette scoffed at her own words and rolled her eyes. "I know," she confessed. "I know how crazy it must sound, but I don't know how else to say it. It's not a dream, Care."

Carrie pulled a long draw of breath through her nose and let it seep out again between a thin gap in her lips.

"The dreams have always been so real," Nicolette explained. "They're always so vivid. I wake up with the words ringing in my ears and the feeling of cold hands still wrapped tightly around my wrists.

They stay with me like nothing else." Nicolette sipped the tea and stared off into a void only she could feel.

"Sometimes dreams are like that," Carrie stated, trying to shorten the gap that was forming between them. "I've had plenty of dreams that have stuck with me for days, or even months."

"It's not like that," Nicolette professed. Her jaw hardened and her cheeks became tense. "It's not a dream, Care."

"I don't understand," Carrie admitted. "How? How is it not a dream?"

"Because it happens all the time." The response was loud and sharp, like an ax splitting a log.

Carrie narrowed her eyes and pursed her lips.

Nicolette scratched at the corner of her mouth and huffed out her irritation. The tea was warm and the smell was soothing, but it didn't seem strong enough for what she currently felt.

"What do you mean?" Carrie asked, trying to draw the truth out of her sister.

Nicolette squeezed the cup with a vigor that was surprising even to her. "It happens," she sputtered, "when I'm awake." The last two words blubbered out in a miserable sob. All of the strength seemed to fall out of her with the confession. "When I'm awake, Care," she repeated. "I see it. I see him. I can feel him in my blood and in my head. He's there, and I can't get rid of him."

"Nicky," Carrie said in a wary tone. "Nicky, you're scaring me a little – all this talk about people in your head. It's scaring me."

Nicolette took a deep breath and looked her big sister in the eye. "It scares me too."

2

DOWNWARD SPIRAL

The sun rose bright over the skyline, filling in the corners and chasing away the shadows of the night. Aaron sipped his cup and watched the sun, smiling as he thought to the sun, 'It's funny how important you are, seeing that if you were any farther away we would all freeze, or any closer and we'd all burn. We need you, but you could kill us all. In the end, I guess you're just like me: hot and dangerous.'

Aaron snickered at his comment and poured a second cup of coffee. Sipping from his own mug and balancing the other from a finger, he made his way across the dining area and down the short hall to Detrick's room. He rapped gently on the door, realizing that it was early but certain that his roommate would be up by then, and waited for an answer. When none came, he gripped both mugs in a single hand and twisted the handle with the other. The shades were drawn low and, except for a thin band of sunlight at the bottom of the window, the room was steeped in darkness. Aaron let the door fall wide open and peered into the gloom.

"Wakey, wakey," he called quietly. "Time to be up already. I have some coffee and it is gorgeous outside. Get your ass out of bed and let's see that winning smile of yours, eh?" Aaron moved to the bed and looked carefully over the mess of covers and pillows. "Deter?" he asked doubtfully, searching the space and squinting at the sheets. "Deter?" A movement by the window caught Aaron's eye and he glanced up to spot Detrick in the corner. He was perched on a chair and he had a notepad over his lap. "Hey," Aaron said happily. "What's up? I have coffee."

Detrick didn't look up from his notepad.

Aaron moved to the window and set the extra coffee on the sill. With a yank, he raised the roller blind and turned to his friend. "I don't want to sound like your mother or anything," he began, pausing for Detrick to make a comment. When none came, Aaron finished his own statement, "But you shouldn't be writing in the dark. It'll hurt your eyes."

Detrick continued to work away at his paper, oblivious to his friend's presence.

"What are you doing?" Aaron finally demanded, looking over the edge of the paper. "What's got your attention so completely?" He looked past Detrick's scribbling hand and at the large dark symbol he was making over the entire paper. Upside-down it looked to Aaron like a curved black snake crawling over the page. "What the hell is that?"

Detrick didn't answer. He scratched his pen over the outline making the image darker and bolder with every stroke. Aaron watched the behavior silently, worried that his roommate was acting a little too fanatical for his taste.

"That's uh... what's that supposed to be?"

Detrick stopped for the first time and looked over his finished picture. "I dunno," he said in a dreamy voice. "I just like it." Detrick slid the paper off his lap and onto the floor. Aaron tracked the picture as it fell and gasped when it hit the floor. The light in the room was growing and Aaron saw that the space around Detrick's chair was covered in discarded papers. Dozens of pages littered the floor, and each of them bearing the same symbol. Over and over it appeared, big and small and light and dark. Some pages bore the symbol multiple times, while others were marked with a single image bold and menacing. As Aaron stood there trying to process it all, Detrick tore another page from his notebook and began again, sketching thick dark lines in black ink.

A̲

It was long past the time when Amanda normally went to bed, but when there was a new book in the house, the hours seemed to slip by faster than any other time. She would sit in her armchair, her knees brought up and tucked to one side and a blanket draped over her, and she would consume a book with dangerous levels of obsessive behavior. Old books. New authors. Historical fiction. Fantasy. There were no favorite genres and no favorite writers when Amanda got like this. Instead, there was only the current book, and in the rest of the world nothing else seemed to burn quite as brightly. To her, it was like falling in love. You would meet, drawn together by a simple glance or a chance phrase. There was an introduction, and with every little piece of information that was shared, the intrigue and attraction would build. She wanted more, with a thirst that seemed impossible to satisfy. So the hours would pass and the feelings would build until finally at long last but usually too soon, the story would be over; the book would be finished. Only after turning the final page and closing the cover, could she come back to her life and move forward. No two books were alike, and no two loves were the same, but the dance never changed.

Until now.

There was something about this time. She knew the experience would be new from the moment the book weighed in her hand at the store. This piece promised to be more than just Amanda falling in love with it, though it seemed capable of returning the feeling somehow. She couldn't quite explain it, and maybe it was because the book was so old. She swore it seemed just as eager to be in her hands as she was to have it there. If it was possible for a book to be alive – if it could yearn and ache and desire – then this book would have been it.

As a story, it progressed differently than any other piece she had read. Partly history, partly memoir, and partly ghost story, the book told the tale of a man that was granted an amazing power but was unaware of what he had. Amanda could only describe the writing as a conversation, and the words demanded that she participate in equal measure. Many times she was left wondering about a portion, asking herself questions and waiting for the author to reply and at each turn, the book obliged and kept the conversation going. She didn't always understand what the book was trying to say, but there seemed to be real effort in the writing to reach out and grab onto her.

And then there were the pictures. They were crude hand drawn images that were more like caricatures than accurate sketches. The men's arms and legs were far too long, and the necks of the women stretched impossibly far. Eyes and noses looked too small to Amanda, and the mouths dominated the faces.

And yet, they were beautiful.

The man in the story, with his tiny black eyes, comically large hands, and his full feminine mouth, still spoke to her heart. She wanted to connect with him. She wanted to understand him. She wanted to be the love in his life.

The lead woman was a miserable creature. By the drawing, you'd expect a polite, kind, soft soul, but just as is true in life, her looks proved to be deceiving. Behind the bright eyes and smooth skin dwelt a monster of a human being; controlling, manipulative, oppressive and hateful. Amanda loathed her name whenever it came on the page, and pleaded with the author to kill her off.

When the moment finally came, it was unlike anything Amanda was prepared to read because it was exactly as she had wished.

The lead in the story, a young and wealthy man named Phillip Rundagger, was set to be married to the daughter of the Dowager Countess, Lady Catherine Sproul. It was not the match Lady Catherine had dreamt of; preferring instead the handsome but poverty-stricken son of the Earl of Marsh, but her family was not to be dissuaded. The plans were made and the date was set. In the background of Phillip's life was an amazing discovery. He had come to learn that he possessed the remarkable ability of capturing life in art, and would spend hours a day drawing items in his journal. When he did so, the item would disappear from the world around him and be trapped within the book. Lady Catherine called him a fool and a liar, insisting that it was nothing more than a child's trick. Her treatment of him worsened and for chapter after chapter Lady Catherine would bemoan the fate of being married to a man that Amanda had come to love and admire. To Amanda, Phillip was energetic, creative, and artful. He was delicate and patient, if not strangely aware of a presence and power no one else could grasp. With each turn of the page, Amanda's adoration grew alongside Lady Catherine's contempt. Finally, halfway through the book, Amanda's fantasy came true.

It crossed her mind that if Phillip could take anything from life and trap it in his book, then he could trap a person just as easily as anything else. When Phillip drew a spider from his window and it disappeared into the book, Amanda became excited that her wish would come true.

But that wasn't enough.

Lady Catherine had been so wicked to Phillip, so hateful and merciless, trapping her in the book would not be enough. Amanda chuckled darkly at the thought of Phillip drawing her disfigured, with twisted limbs and a contorted face. As the thought tickled her, Amanda then imagined Phillip dividing the body of Lady Catherine in the book so that she would forever be trapped in a state of misery and torture.

It was an especially morbid thought for the normally quiet and peaceful lady, but she entertained it nonetheless. Amanda figured her musings were harmless.

It was, after all, just a book.

She read on as Phillip reached the end of his patience and saw no way out for himself. In a desperate and wicked act, the man drew his fiancé into the book. He first drew her face, contorted and screaming in pain, just as Amanda had pictured. The imagery came hard, fast, and exciting. So much so that Amanda was caught up in the rush of reading her ideas come to life that she didn't pause to think of the darkness in the idea. She gasped when Phillip drew an arm next – detached from the body. The other limbs as well were drawn, mangled, and separate, with a torso floating in the middle of the page. When he finished, Phillip looked on with a strange and brooding satisfaction.

And then the screams began.

Wails and shrieks echoed through the Dowager's manor, filling the halls and digging into the mind. The noise grew to unimaginable heights until Phillip feared the noise would make him insane. On and on, the cry of the dying blasted through the house longer than any living breath could sustain. The butler threw himself from a window for the sound of it and the footmen began to beat one another. The maids cowered and wept, but the Dowager Countess lied in the stillness of her bed, immobile and silent through the episode.

And then it stopped. The voice simply cut out like a string breaking or a lid snapping shut. It was there one moment, beating, piercing, and horrible, and in a blink, it was gone. The butler lay dead. The maids wept. The footmen collapsed. The Dowager Countess remained frozen. Phillip Rundagger took his hands from his ears and slowly opened his eyes. On the floor was his book, open to his image of Lady Catherine. The image was just a rough sketch, yet it became so vivid, and so horrid. As he watched, it seemed to move so slightly, the image on the page, and it became wet. Blood seeped from the dry paper and a thin line of the red life poured over the edge of the book and stained the carpet.

Amanda looked at the words and felt as though she had been struck in the face by a winter wind. It was her very wish, alive and recorded forever, only more horrible than she could have possibly imagined. Phillip wallowed and suffered on the page, and Amanda was with him. She felt the hurt, heard the scream in her head, and was weighed with the same regret. In one stroke she was both more enamored than ever and more embarrassed than she thought possible.

And the book was only halfway done.

The clock on her phone read two in the morning, but her eyelids were as light as if it was midday. Within their cage, her heart beat against her ribs and her lungs panted and pressed against her sides. It was all too much, she decided, but when she moved to put the book away, her hand wouldn't obey.

Just one more page.

Amanda flipped the paper and stared at the heading for the next section. The art had changed and the font was completely different. If Amanda had not known any better, she would have thought that two books had been stitched together under a single cover. But there was Phillip's name heading the first sentence, and the mention of his sketchbook. It was as though the entire story was about to change. Amanda's practical side repeated that this would be the perfect time to stop, but the reader within begged for the next adventure. As she debated, Amanda's eyes drifted to the top of the page and saw a strange symbol. It looked like an old Celtic or Norse letter, only it was rounded and wrapped around itself. She didn't know what it meant, but she knew it was Phillip. Her fingertips dragged lightly over the page, tracing the lines like a mother strokes the hair of her child. In an instance, a peaceful drowsiness crept up and slipped its arms around her. As the spell took hold, Amanda found that she could no longer keep her eyes open. Reluctantly at first, but with an increasing willingness, Amanda let the book fall closed and she rose from her chair. She then walked, slowly and happily down the hall and to her bed, knowing that tomorrow the second half of the story of the mirrors would bring just as much joy and mystery as the first.

In a single sitting, it had become more than a book to Amanda. It was the life of a dear friend, and she couldn't wait to see how it ended.

She opened it again first thing in the morning, right after visiting her bathroom. The book had consumed her every moment, and Amanda was in danger of purposefully leaving her life on hold until the last page had turned.

The murder of Phillip Rundagger's fiancé left him emotionally crippled. He locked himself away in his home, cloistered from friends, family, and society at large. Of course the discussions in the parlors around the county suggested that the man was simply too distraught after the violent disappearance of the woman who was to be the joy of his life. Her body was never recovered of course, leaving behind only a room that had been torn apart and stained with blood, which only increased the sympathy of his friends and neighbors. No one faulted Rundagger for withdrawing, though not one of the steady stream of well-wishers had any idea the truth of that night.

Phillip Rundagger was a murderer.

The kind, soft, quiet artist at the beginning of the book had been transformed. Amanda read his thoughts with a gently breaking heart. She felt connected to him, and knew that he was not a killer. Phillip was a gentle man that had made a terrible mistake, and by doing so had released something dark inside him that he was no longer able to control. A piece of him, dark and brooding and primal, has been released, and now Rundagger had to find a way to overcome the wave of violent thoughts and dreams that were consuming him. Every word of the story pulled Amanda further from her own life and buried her within the seven mirrors, until the true terror became evident.

Phillip Rundagger was dying.

The man she had met and loved in the first half of the book was disappearing one line at a time. He was no longer a soft soul in a difficult world; Rundagger was becoming a monster, and there was only one thing that could protect him.

At the height of his isolation, when Philip was doing everything he could to protect the world from the creature he had become, the tortured soul began to draw a simple rune on a piece of paper. It was like something from antiquity, a basic line that looped over itself in curving pattern. The shape gave him a sense of peace. The shape gave him a sense of security. He started drawing the symbol on every scrap of paper he had allowed in his self-made cell. When the paper ran out, he drew it on the desk, and then the walls, and then the floor. Philip drew the symbol until he no longer had ink in the well. He then moved to paint, and plastered the rune boldly over the walls and ceiling. He painted the floor, the rug, his bed-spread, and he painted it even on himself. The more he drew the symbol the better he felt. The peace that came with the protection of the mark was intoxicating, and Philip swore to himself that he would never be without it. He would commission the jeweler to fash-ion a golden necklace of the symbol so that when the ink and the paint wore off his skin, he would still forever be covered with the precious symbol. It was to be the only thing that could restore his soul, and Rundagger wanted it to be with him, always.

Time stood still and Amanda forgot what she was doing. When her mind rejoined the world, Amanda blinked hard and shook her head clear. She slipped her hand to the nightstand and pulled an empty coffee mug from under the glow of the lamp. Amanda huffed at the sight and checked the time.

It was twenty after eleven.

Since waking, Amanda had only left her bed to pour a cup of cof-fee and make one quick stop in the bathroom, and both had been done with the book in her hands. As much as she didn't want to admit it, her day was going by quickly and nothing has been accomplished.

"The price of a good book," she said philosophically.

Amanda looked around her bedroom and stretched her arms above her head, letting out a long and satisfied growl. Her legs drifted over the edge of her bed and she stood for the first time in hours, scratching her stomach through her shirt and blinking slowly at herself in the mirror. "You," she said to her reflection in the mirror, "need a shower and a bite to eat."

While getting cleaned up and ready to go out, Amanda found herself painting the symbol from the book on random objects with a dry finger. She drew it in the air and in the fog of a post-shower bathroom mirror. She practiced the symbol on the counter in the kitchen and even lightly scratched the mark on her own arm. The subtle red glow of irritated skin made the rune look as though it was something emerging from inside her. The thought made her laugh.

When Amanda was ready to go out, she decided to take the book with her. There would undoubtedly be a line at the coffee shop and that would give her a chance to get a few more pages in. She would have felt silly explaining the way the book affected her, but that didn't stop her from driving a little faster than normal. She didn't expect everyone to love a good story the way she did, and this book had absolutely possessed her in a way she never could have imagined. The only strange part was that she wanted it to. Amanda tried not to think about the why, but she knew that this book was vital. The man trapped in its pages had become like a dear friend, and until she learned the fate of this man, she was willing to completely give herself to the story.

<u>M</u>

Michaela sat in her booth, the smell of fast food wafting up from her table. The cheeseburger sat on its paper wrapper and the fries cooled in the little cardboard cup. A thin cup of soda sweat a ring onto the table, but Michaela saw none of this. She had her phone on and at arm's length in front of her with the camera pointed back at her chest. In the little screen, she studied her fresh tattoo: red, swollen, and seeping. A bandage hung loosely over the deep cut of her shirt, a single piece of tape holding it to her pale skin, and it was spotted with little dots of blood and black marks. The artist had told her to keep it covered and she had obeyed, but Michaela could not contain herself any longer. She had to see it.

Michaela had first drawn the image on a whim. She was bored, and as she often did when there was nothing else to do, she had started doodling on the first thing she could lay her hands on. It was a receipt that had been riding around in her pocket for the last couple of days. The first time she drew it, the symbol now permanently etched above her breasts, Michaela knew it was perfect. She flipped the receipt and then drew it on the other side. Then on her hand. Then on a piece of junk mail. Over and over she drew it, and each time it was exactly the same. It was perfect, just the way it was. Regardless of where it appeared or what she used to create it, the image just seemed complete. In any medium and on any surface, she could look upon the image and there was a sense of peace and a sense of perfection.

Despite all that, when Michaela brought the picture to the artist and he put her idea down permanently, there was still a piece of her that was worried it wouldn't bring her the same level of satisfaction. Staring into her phone, she no longer had any doubts. The tattoo seemed to glow upon her chest with a soft purple light. She knew it was just a trick with the camera on her phone, but Michaela still took it as a sign that the image was meant to be. She didn't know why, or how, or to what it would lead, but Michaela was certain that the marking would be significant to her for the rest of her life. Until she died, every day, she was positive she would never regret this tattoo.

"Miss?"

Michaela watched the image on the phone; fascinated that something so beautiful could last forever.

"Miss?"

She looked up slowly, her head feeling as though it was filled with sand for some strange reason, and looked into the eyes of the employee standing over her.

"Miss, are you okay?" the female employee asked.

Michaela watched the face of the employee with a calm disinterest. The colorful polo shirt dotted with grease and the dirty ponytails were bad enough by themselves, but Michaela was offended most that the person interrupting her was also in her forties. As far as she was concerned, anyone still frying food for a living in their forties had no business telling her anything. Michaela made a face that communicated as much and tried to look back at her screen.

"Miss," the employee continued, "do you need a doctor?"

The question caught Michaela by surprise. "Why?" she asked, irritation building. Michaela's eyes darted back to the forty year-olds face. The concern filling the employee's eyes and the panic that was painted over the faces of gawking customers made Michaela want to punch someone. What was wrong with them? What was the matter with these people?

Michaela tipped her phone to see her face in the camera and regretted it immediately.

Grey.

The image on the screen was the face of a skeleton. Her eyes were sunken and her skin was pulled taunt. Her hair was thinning and her neck looked gaunt and brittle. The tip of Michaela's nose glowed pink and there was a dark line tracing the edge of her lips.

She looked dead.

Michaela looked back up at the employee and finally understood the alarm in her eyes. "What's happening to me?" Michaela managed. "What's going on?" She pushed off from the table and rose to her feet.

"Maybe you should stay seated," the employee suggested.

Michaela wasn't listening though. Her legs felt like they had turned to wood and her arms were like windsocks, tossed about and weak. She staggered for a moment while she worked to keep her balance, but she was certain that the faintest breeze would send her to the floor.

"Miss," the employee said as Michaela made her way to the front of the lobby. "Miss?"

Michaela stumbled and tripped her way past the crowd, alarmed by how quickly people jumped to get out of the way. It was as though she was radioactive; as if no one wanted to risk even touching her for fear that the death that was taking the poor girl would consume them next.

Ignoring the looks and the muttered comments, Michaela steered herself to the restroom and to a sink. She needed to see it for herself, without the camera, in the clear and honest reflection of a mirror. She lurched to the nearest counter and looked into the mirror before she lost her nerve, and what she found made Michaela raise her hand to her face and touch it carefully.

She was beautiful.

The image in the glass was smooth with healthy skin. Her hair was thick, rich, and full. Her lips were large and full of color, just like her eyes. There was a glow in her cheeks and neck, and her posture looked better than ever. Everything about her, from the way her clothes fit to the shape of her hips and bust, looked amazing. It was unbelievable. It was astounding. It was a dream come to life. Finally, she was that girl.

Michaela stepped away from the counter and looked down at herself. Clean strong hands rotated before her eyes with strong healthy nails and hairless arms. There were no wrinkles. There was no sun damage. There were no moles, spots, blemishes, or scars. She was perfect. She was immaculate. She was unbelievable.

"Miss?" The voice of the employee was immediately recognizable. Michaela ran her fingers through her luscious hair as the worker asked, "Is everything okay?"

Michaela stepped away from the sink and enjoyed the terrified look on the woman's face. "Oh yeah," she answered. "Everything is perfect."

O

The sun on his face and the breeze on his neck was the greatest feeling Orin could remember. He strolled down the sidewalk, dragging his fingers in the leaves of the low branches above him and humming to himself like a man released without a care in the world. He hadn't eaten in almost two days, and yet Orin felt stronger and more energized than ever. He breathed deeply, hopping onto a nearby bench and looking out over the cars that passed slowly on the downtown avenue. One by one, the cars went by, and one by one, he watched them go.

None of it mattered. There was no life anymore. There was no death. He couldn't explain it if he tried, but the young man now knew he was somehow past the worries and the anxieties of normal life. From here on out, there was nothing but life and the experiences that came with it.

He slipped from the bench and landed smoothly on his feet. Orin moved casually, allowing the wind to guide him wherever it would, never looking back and never questioning a step. The world around him was wide, bright and free.

He remembered the looks on the faces of the doctors in the emergency room. He remembered how the nurses tried to get him to go back into his bed. He could still hear the voice of the doctor ordering someone to call the police for some reason. Couldn't they see? He was finally alive. Years of living in the dark. Years of questioning who he was. A life spent hiding his face and covering his mouth, and for what? To be cast aside? Looked over? Ignored and forgotten?

Not anymore.

Orin had simply walked out. No one wanted to touch him, and why should they? He was no longer like them – the doctors and the nurses and the rest of the people in the hospital. Those men and women surrounded themselves with death and sickness all day. Orin was now alive, and more so than they would ever be. In the end, the people in the hospital just watched him as he walked away, over the parking lot and down the street.

He rounded a corner and spied a group of adults standing in a circle, talking about nothing, and ignoring the life that was happening around them. Standing outside the circle and looking bored was a little boy who looked seven or eight to Orin. He strolled up close, sneaking along to avoid the attention of the adults, and he waved to the child. The little boy looked up wearily and Orin gave him a wink. "Wanna see a magic trick?" he asked the child. The little boy looked around and then nodded. Orin pulled his sleeve back and the child's face was bathed in purple light.

N

The night was growing outside the glass of the window, and the bay was gently glowing under the lights of a boulevard and the boardwalk. The waves rolled in and pressed silently against the wood and stone of the pier, and a small boat cruised lightly over the water. Men and women stood along the rails and children tossed stones in the water, recreating the same movements countless people had made since humans first wandered to the edge of our dry world. There was nothing new outside. Everything was on a loop, playing the same images and sounds one generation after the next. There were no surprises in life for those who watched carefully, Nicolette thought to herself. Seated at the edge of the bed; she looked out over a world that was beyond impressing her. There was nothing new outside. There was only what was within.

The moon was all but invisible in the soft red and orange of the sunset. The clouds were thick to the east and far to the west, but the sky over the gulf was as clear as a picture. The south was a sheet of blue sky and rolling purple waves. White caps danced and peeked over the surface, and the last swimmers and beachers of the day pushed out, wasting none of the remaining light. The sight was at once alive and still; it was fresh and yet remarkably familiar. It used to be that Nicolette would look out her window and she could feel the stresses of the day drop off like water and evaporate at her feet. There was nothing that a few moments looking at the seas couldn't fix.

Until now.

The dreams were worse than ever. In the beginning, Nicolette would wake violently in her bed, shrouded in the dark of the night and dripping with sweat. Her muscles would ache the next day and she would smile at the thought of all the inadvertent exercise she was receiving. But then the dreams became more regular. They were coming every night, sometimes more than once. Horrifying images would drag her from sleep, only to be waiting for her once she was again unconscious. Night after night, it went on. She called her friends, but no one listened. They told her to take melatonin, to drink tea, or to avoid electronics before bed. They told her to do yoga, or stretching, or meditation to calm her mind. Her friends gave her loads of advice, but no one understood.

Nicolette was not having trouble sleeping.

She was having troubles with her mind.

Carrie seemed to be the only one that cared, but she had no solutions either. Her suggestions sounded like everyone else's. Eat this. Drink that. Do this. Don't do that. All of it was well-meaning, but none of it helped.

When the vision started coming in the daylight, Nicolette knew it was more than just her dreams. She knew it had to be her. She confessed to her sister that the visions were not just coming at night, and the reaction was exactly what Nicolette feared. It was the next day when the doctor's office called. They wanted to speak with Nicolette, and asked to make some time in her schedule. The office called and left three messages, and Nicolette deleted each one. She didn't need a doctor to tell her that she was crazy.

Frankly, she already knew that there was something wrong with her. What she needed was for the visions to stop. What she needed was for him to go away.

Him. The one in the vision. The man in the shadow. The eyes.

The light outside faded quickly as the sun disappeared over the hills on the far side of the bay. Nicolette could feel her body longing for sleep but her mind no longer allowed it. It had been almost two days since she had slept, and her body was beginning to feel like a rag that had been used and wrung out, then draped over a rod and left to dry. The night was coming on, and she knew sleep would soon follow. The only desire that matched her urge to sleep was her desperation to stay awake; to stay away from the eyes in the shadow. He came to her in the day, and owned her at night.

As the light in the room grew brighter than the world outside, Nicolette's reflection appeared before her in the glass. Her face was blurry and sunken, with dark caves for eyes and a neutral face. Beneath her was the bed, and behind her was shadow. Tall and looming, growing deeper as the night developed, the shadow took on a new and strange shape.

He was waiting for her.

Eyes in the shadow.

She felt hopeless. There was no escaping him. No matter what she did or where she went, Nicolette knew that he would be there, waiting in the shadow. There was only one escape, but Nicolette was not yet prepared to open her window, look over the ledge to the ground five stories below, and take that final step. She couldn't do it, and it made her feel all the more helpless. She couldn't do it... yet.

In the glass, a new image appeared. It was a shape, like a thick line drawn in curves and crossing over itself to make a rune of some kind. She didn't know what it was, but the sight of the symbol reflected in the glass gave her peace. It appeared exactly on the spot where her face was, like a mask. She felt drawn to it, now painted boldly on the window with such clarity that Nicolette was certain it could be seen from the street. And as she watched in the glass, the shadow behind her faded. The eyes blinked and were gone, and the symbol gave her hope. The rune filled Nicolette with warmth and made her feel alive. She laid back to let the night in and let sleep consume her.

3

OBSESSIONS

D

Amanda slipped from the car and pointed her toes at the entrance to the coffee shop. The book was cracked open and lying in her palms before she reached the door. She reached out and pulled the handle without taking her eyes from the pages. When the door came to a sudden stop Amanda's eyes snapped up. "Oh my god!" she gushed at the young man with his hand on the door. "I am so sorry. Did I get you?"

"Almost," he said in an understanding voice.

"I am so sorry," Amanda repeated, closing her book around her finger and biting her lip.

"Relax," the man replied with a smile. "Almost everyone in my family is a bookworm. I'm very used to the hazards of being around a person whose attention is trapped in a world on paper and not in the world around them." Amanda made a face and her smile flickered. "I'm sorry," the man blushed. "That came out bad. What I meant was that I understand and that I'm not bothered."

Amanda looked over the young man and tried not to laugh as he became progressively more uncomfortable. "Thank you for your understanding."

"Wow," he laughed. "I am really messing this up."

"Are you?" she replied lightly.

"Yeah," he huffed. "I mean, I've got a pretty girl here," the young man added, gesturing towards her, "She's smart and has great taste in coffee," he added, pointing into the shop, "and I am scaring her."

"A little," Amanda teased.

"Well," he sighed, fighting to keep his pride, "I guess there is just one thing left."

"And that is?" Amanda said, amused by the man's awkward manner.

"Hi," he said, holding out his hand. "I'm Detrick."

"Amanda," she said, taking his hand.

"Amanda," he said in gentle and long notes. "Nice to meet you."

"Likewise, Detrick," Amanda replied.

"Hey," a voice called from behind her. Amanda turned and stared at the irritated expression of a middle-aged man. "Can you two make goo-goo eyes at each other somewhere else?" the man asked harshly. "Preferably not in a spot where you're blocking the door?"

"We weren't..." Amanda sputtered.

"Of course," Detrick replied quickly. He stood back and held the door open wide. The man rudely pushed his way past them and took a place in the queue. Detrick bobbed his eyebrows and presented an open hand to Amanda. "After you."

She nodded like a fine lady from a time long passed and moved in behind the rude man waiting in line. As she did so, Amanda noticed a notepad in Detrick's hand. "Are you a writer?"

"No," he laughed. "Why?" She made eyes at the notebook and he made a face that was painted with embarrassment. "This? No. I'm not a writer. Are you kidding? Spending my life at a computer instead of out among the people I would write about? No. That's not me."

"So what is it about," she pressed, "if I can ask?"

"I'm no artist, but I've been drawing a bit lately."

"Really?" she asked.

"Yeah," he said, staring at his shoes. "I've really only been drawing one thing. I just want it to be perfect, you know?"

"Yeah," Amanda answered, waving her book at him. "I know just what you mean."

"Why are you smiling?" Detrick asked nervously.

"You just sound like the guy in this book, that's all," she explained, thinking back to Philip Rundagger, who was drawing the symbol relentlessly, to gather strength from it. "He had been drawing the same thing over and over too. It's odd, you know?" Amanda pointed out. "It's like having the character come to life."

"Do you like him?" Detrick asked.

"The guy in the book?" Amanda clarified.

"The crazy one drawing the same thing over and over."

Amanda couldn't help but notice that Detrick's eyes scanned around the room while he asked. This gave the handsome young man a level of vulnerability she had not seen in so long, Amanda almost didn't recognize it. She waited until Detrick dared to look her in the face before she said, "I do. Immensely."

"There's hope yet," Detrick grinned.

They went on talking about their readings and awkward situations they experienced, which quickly led Detrick to confess what his friend; Aaron dared to ask of him - spying on his girlfriend as an undercover gay person. Amanda covered her mouth and tried to stifle her laugh, though it was no use.

"You're gonna make a guy think that he can't be honest with a lady if you treat him like that," Detrick gently warned. He looked around the coffee house and nodded to the nosey faces that had all turned to see what the commotion was about.

"I'm sorry," Amanda giggled, still trying to hide her face. "I'm sorry. Really."

"You sound sorry," Detrick teased, tapping the bottom of his empty coffee mug against the wooden table and smiling kindly at

Amanda. His eyes were soft and warm, and the red in his cheeks made them look even more so at the moment.

"Don't be embarrassed," Amanda said, smiling brightly. "But that can't be true."

"It is," Detrick assured her. "Aaron is madly in love with this girl, but he doesn't trust her."

"So he asked you to be his date?" Amanda clarified. "I don't get it. Why did he want you to pose as his boyfriend?"

"He didn't," Detrick explained, giving a look to the older couple at the nearest table. "He wasn't going. He just wanted me to spy for him."

"By pretending to be gay?" Amanda giggled. "At least he didn't ask you to dress in drag."

"I thought he did at first," Detrick admitted.

"Oh no!" Amanda blurted, again covering her mouth in shock.

"What's the big deal?" Detrick asked with a droll grin. "Can't picture me in a dress?"

"Is it bad that I assumed you would be in a miniskirt?" she asked in a restrained voice.

Detrick laughed and again tapped his cup on the table. "There's nothing wrong if that's your thing, but there was no way I was spying for him."

"Sounds like Aaron doesn't love her as much as he thinks he does," Amanda commented, picking up her coffee and taking a sip.

"What? No," Detrick answered. "He loves Jessica. He just gets a little jealous sometimes is all." Amanda hummed to herself and looked at the tabletop. "Honestly," Detrick pressed. "He's a good guy."

"I'm sure he is," Amanda said with an appeasing look in her eye.

"But you think he doesn't trust her, so he doesn't really love her?"

"I don't mean to pick a fight," Amanda offered.

"And I don't feel attacked," Detrick said pleasantly. "Not at all. It's just that I don't often hear an observation that is so different from my own and yet still makes perfect sense."

Amanda could feel her skin flush and she looked away in embarrassment. She wasn't used to accepting compliments, and that was especially true when it came from a handsome men she had just met. "Shut up," she chided herself in her thoughts, turning her attention out the window. Once she was certain that she wouldn't make a fool of herself, Amanda turned her eyes back to Detrick and tried to hold a straight face.

"So?" Detrick prompted.

"So." Amanda answered.

"Aaron needs a new girlfriend, then?" he stated.

"Aaron needs to figure out what is causing his issues and he needs to fix that before he starts getting worried by anything his girlfriend does," Amanda said flatly. "Because chances are the real problem is with him. He needs to figure that out first. After that he can reevaluate his girlfriend, and I'm willing to bet the problem he thought was there, no longer is."

Everything she said made sense to Detrick, who watched her with a reverential grin. "Where were you the other day?"

"Around," she answered coyly, sipping from her coffee.

"You are clearly a more insightful person than I am," Detrick complimented.

"Not necessarily," she hurriedly replied.

"It makes me want to ask you all sorts of things, just to see what kind of magic you're capable of."

"Like why you're drawing the same picture over and over?" Amanda said teasingly. Detrick tried to smile but it was clear that she had struck a nerve. She immediately apologized but an invisible line had already been crossed.

"Don't worry about it," he said dismissively. "It's just me being a little nuts that's all."

"I think it's a sign of creativity."

"I don't think so," Detrick insisted, hanging his head. "It's a little worse than that."

"Really?" she smiled. "Plenty of professional artists study a subject for months, drawing and painting and practicing the same form over and over. They'll draw the same thing hundreds of times."

"Can we talk about something else?" Detrick asked.

Amanda sat back in her chair and made a concerned face. "Sure. Sorry."

"I'm not... I'm sorry," Detrick fumbled, pulling his phone from his pocket. "It was really nice meeting you."

He looked at the screen and shrugged his shoulders. "I've got to run. I really am glad to have shared a table with you. Thank you."

"Yeah," Amanda replied, watching Detrick move toward the door. As the door closed behind him Amanda commented in a small voice, "...but apparently you didn't have a good enough time to ask for my number."

She finished her coffee in a drink and waited just long enough to ensure that there was no chance Detrick was still in the parking lot. She then rose from her seat and picked up her coat and book. Amanda then strolled to the door, trying desperately to look as though she didn't just run off the first attractive man to take an interest in her in over a year.

A

The trip home was a short and silent one with only two thoughts surviving in her head. The first was that there was no way she would ever see that man again. After freaking him out over his art, something he was clearly sensitive talking about, if he ever saw her again Amanda was positive that he would turn and run as fast as he did that morning.

The second thought was her book. It seemed to call to her the entire drive back to the house, promising that all she need for a quiet mind was a hot cup of tea and an hour reading. So, when Amanda parked the car there was no conscious decision to rush in the front door and fill the kettle. She had resorted to autopilot, knowing that this was the only thing that would make her feel better. As the kettle heated, she kicked her shoes off and picked up the book. The cover opened easily in her hand and the pages split and flopped apart. She gazed for several moments at the open page and the image at the top.

It was the rune.

The second half had taken a decidedly dark turn, though Amanda was not put off. She was no stranger to stories that worked at a person's fears and had no trouble with reading about shocking and atrocious events. She could always fall back in the comfort of knowing that it was only a story, and her feelings are just the product of reading the work of a gifted storyteller. That was also the reason she never read true crime stories or any biographies of killers. Amanda mainly read for the enjoyment and connection with the author, not to be terrified of shopping alone. So, as she read about Rundagger and the transformation he experienced, she could at least tell herself that regardless of the emotions that were stirred, it was, in the end, just a story. And yet, no matter how many times Amanda reminded herself of that point, repeating the declaration over and over as the pages flipped past, she was unable to shake the thought that there was more happening here than she knew. The more she read the less it felt like some story, and the more it felt like her own story.

If the book was a play in three acts, then the first half was some strange mixture of romance, comedy, and horror. The evolution of the man she had come to admire, Phillip Rundagger, left her out of breath and with more questions than she knew how to answer.

And in that moment, Amanda saw the man she had loved in the beginning of the book, slowly being born again under the power of the symbol. Philip had all his body covered in the faded, distorted markings, but the weight, the confident glow of the golden necklace granted the peace he was looking for desperately. Philip Rundagger became a changed man, but the symbol showed the way out, from the darkness of the torments he had to endure.

Amanda flipped back to the beginning of the section and again looked at the symbol at the top of the page. It was such a simple and unassuming mark, then her heartbeat faster for having looked upon it. The rune was more than just some ink on an old page; it had become the symbol of Philip's recovery, and Amanda felt her own connection to the shape. The book would end and her life would go on, but that shape will still have saved Philip and changed her life. Once again, she found her fingertips tracing the loops and curves.

<u>M</u>

Smoke rose up from Michaela's lips as she leaned against a pickup parked at the small park, downtown. She had her feet planted on the sidewalk and her eyes on her reflection in the shop window before her. Michaela watched herself, propped up against the hood of the sleek truck, one hand stretched out behind her and the other dangling to one side. Her black tank top hung loosely over her thin frame while her grey skirt lied limply over her bare legs. A pair of black ankle boots with heels completed the outfit, making her stand out like an anorexic at fat camp. She flicked her cigarette between her fingers and let the sunglasses sag down the bridge of her nose. There was an air of indifference in everything that she did which caught the eye of most men walking by. It was a new sensation for her – being the article of public attention – but the quiet girl didn't give it much thought. The last two days had been like emerging from a shell that was nineteen years old. The world was all new, and while nothing seemed to make sense anymore none of it seemed to matter either. The world was a small and silly toy, and Michaela was determined to have the greatest time she could manage. So when the good old boys would stroll past and whistle or comment, Michaela paid them an equal amount of respect by looking them up and down, then ignoring them completely. If nothing else, she wanted the catcallers to know that she gave them some thought and found the men wholly disappointing.

"Well hello, little miss," a deep southern voice said happily. Michaela turned her eyes to find a tall man with faded blue jeans and a tight flannel shirt sauntering up to her. He had a worn out baseball cap on his head of a team she didn't recognize and a pair of dusty lace up boots on his feet. "I've seen some things decorating the hood of my truck before," the man announced with a proud smile, "but I ain't never seen nothin' up there as pretty as you."

"Really?" Michaela asked in a bored tone.

"No miss, I haven't," the man assured her.

Michaela pinched her cigarette between her lips and planted one heel on the bumper. As the man smiled and watched, she pushed herself up and sat properly on the hood of the pickup. "Now imagine that," Michaela asked, pulling the cigarette from her lips and tapping a small pile of ash onto the shiny paint. The man made an uncomfortable face at the sight but said nothing. "You think I'm pretty."

It wasn't a question. The tone would have matched a person calling a crayon colorful or saying that a stone was hard. Michaela was repeating a fact, and she sounded utterly disenchanted by the idea.

"Why yes I do," the man agreed, stepping close and resting his elbow on the hood. He leaned in and gave her his best country boy smile. "How about you and I go for a little spin, huh?" the man suggested. "I'll take you out to a place with an amazing view, then you and I can get a bite to eat somewhere."

Michaela looked over what she figured was a man at least ten years older than her, and likely more. His face was soft and round, but his body was tall and thin. He had dark hair peeking out from under his hat and soft blue eyes. Looking into his face, Michaela wanted nothing more than to jam her cigarette in his mouth.

"So what do ya say, hmm?" he pressed, drawing lines on the metal beside her leg. "Wanna go for a spin?"

Michaela took a long drag off her cigarette and blew a column of smoke into the air. "Yeah," she said as though the answer wasn't all that important.

"Well hot damn," the man replied coolly, rising off the hood. "Then let's hit it."

Michaela held out her hand and the man moved to help her down. "Nuh-uh," she corrected, moving her hand from his and holding out her palm.

"What are you doing?" the man laughed.

"I just wanna go for a little ol' ride," Michaela answered in a trashy southern belle accent. "That's all."

The man squinted and smiled, trying to keep track of what she could mean. "So let's go then," he said patiently.

"No," Michaela replied, her hand still out and open. "At least not with you."

A snort left the man's nose as he looked at the girl perched on his truck. "Not with me?" he said, laughing at the statement. "Honey, that's kind of the deal, see? My truck. My ride. If you wanna come along then I would be more than happy to have ya. I'll show you a real nice time, and hell, I'll even take you out for a couple drinks after. So if you wanna go, then slide that cute little butt of yours off my truck and let's hit it."

"No," Michaela answered in the same bored tone.

"Girl," the man said, irritation rising in his voice, "I don't think I get you."

"Clearly not," she responded, smiling for the first time. "You see, I want your truck. Not you."

The cowboy looked around and laughed aloud. His eyes scanned for an audience but found that no one was close enough to hear their conversation. "Well what you don't get," he said, turning back to

Michaela, "is that we're a package deal, see? The truck and me? She doesn't go anywhere I don't, and nobody drives this truck but me. So if you're lookin' to leave in this pickup," he added, lowering his voice and moving himself between her knees, "then you are leavin' here with me. And I don't mind sayin' we are going to have a good old time, you and me."

"I don't think so," Michaela decided, adding to the pile of ash beside her. The man's eyes flared indignantly. He pulled a handkerchief from his pocket and swiped the ash to the concrete. "You're going to give me the keys to this truck," Michaela continued nonchalantly, "and then you are going to turn around and leave."

"Or maybe," the man growled, "you're gonna to get your ass in the truck." He laid a hand on her thigh and squeezed her until his knuckles were white. Michaela looked on curiously. "No little city girl is gonna play the slut with me and then back down like that. Ask for my truck? Ha! I'd sooner shoot my dog."

"But kidnapping and rape aren't a problem?" Michaela asked, genuinely amused.

"You ain't my dog, are ya?" the man said in a quiet snarl. "And this ain't no kidnappin' neither. You're just doin' what you implied and I am keeping ya honest. Now get in the truck before I bust you in the head and put you there." His fingernails dug into her skin as he twisted and tightened his grip on her leg. Michaela puffed the last of her cigarette and put it out on the hood of the truck. "And take care of the paint ya little floozy."

She breathed out a thin line of smoke and smiled at the man. "Finally," she said calmly. "Some fun."

Michaela slipped her arms over the man's shoulders and let her hands rest limply over this back. The man tensed and looked around, confused by her apparent willingness. She lolled her head off to one side and stared into his rage-filled eyes. Michaela slid a hand to the back of his head and pulled him in for a long kiss. His grip on her leg loosened and moved up her thigh. She responded, kissing him harder and moaning into his mouth. The cowboy shuffled himself deeper between her legs and pressed his free hand to the small of her back. She arched and he let out a hungry groan. Michaela fluttered her eyes and looked behind the cowboy. Standing along the wall was a tall black man, watching it all.

He had on a black t-shirt and a pair of skinny black jeans. His sneakers were old, but the tattoo on the outside of his forearm was brand new.

And it looked exactly like Michaela's.

He pulled a cigarette from behind his ear and snapped his fingers. A small flame appeared between his forefinger and thumb, and he held the little fire to the rolled stick of tobacco. Michaela watched with a sparkle in her eye.

The cowboy's moans became longer and his eyes began to flicker. His grip became loose and his muscles relaxed, until it seemed that he would fall over at any moment. At that point, as the man teetered and buckled, Michaela pushed him away slightly and popped her lips. "Keys," she said.

The cowboy looked back at her with a vacant stare. With slow and sloppy movements, he dug his car keys from his pocket and placed them in her waiting hand. His skin was beginning to look sickly and sweat was forming around his brow.

"You should go lay down," Michaela whispered to him. "Find a bench in the park and take a nap." Without a word, the cowboy stumbled back like a foal before toddling down the sidewalk on his own. She watched him leave without any great feelings. He would certainly be an easy victim for anyone that came across him, especially now that Michaela had drained the will right out of him, but in a way, she felt that was poetic. "With any luck," she mumbled happily, "some good old boy will offer him a ride out to the woods somewhere and he can have his own good time." She slipped from the hood of the truck and opened the driver door. She then tossed the keys to the man in the black tee and gave him an expectant look. "Michaela," she announced.

"Orin," the young man replied.

Michaela scooted over the bench and into the passenger seat before lighting another cigarette.

Orin strolled casually over and sat behind the wheel. He pulled the driver door lovingly, and pulled it in just hard enough to close it securely. He ran his hand along the wood trim interior and over the wooden steering wheel. The console lighted with a digital display as he turned the key, and the powerful motor under the hood roared to life.

"What kind of truck is it?" Michaela asked, watching how gently Orin did everything.

"Heck if I know," he replied with a straight face. He pulled the gearshift into reverse and backed out of the parking spot. For a moment, Orin sat in the middle of the street, watching a reflection of himself and Michaela in the storefront windows. A smile grew over his lips and he nodded to his copilot. "Wanna jack this town up?"

"Do I," she answered, pushing her sunglasses tight against her face.

Orin dropped the truck into drive and stomped on the gas. Engine noise and a loud squeal filled the street while smoke rose from the back as the tires spun freely over the pavement. The truck drifted to one side a few feet before the tires caught and sent the car barreling down the avenue. Orin smiled, steering smoothly and confidently as he and Michaela sped on their way to the edge of town.

O

Jake pushed his scooter again, with a loose kick, rolling down the sidewalk. The scooter had a tiny light on the handlebars, though he purposefully left it switched off. With his hoodie up, he rolled down the street silently, and parked the scooter in the shade of a tree in front of Mr. Wilkins' house.

Mr. Wilkins' pride and joy, the silver Cayenne hybrid parked on the garage driveway, as usual. The sun already disappeared behind the hills. Jake carefully circled around the white spots of the street-lights after he got the plastic bottle out from his backpack.

Jake always thought that he should follow the orders of grownups. When Mr. Wilkins chased him and his buddies away, again and again, from his house front, they accepted their fate. It was the only decent spot in the nearby streets to play a quick 3v3 match with his neighboring friends and soccer teammates. Reaching the playground or the park required a short trip, not something you can just wedge in, if you have a few minutes before homework, dinner, or a quick morning blast before school. Jake asked his father about it, and he said that they have to respect Mr. Wilkins' demands. He promised Jake that he will talk to him, but none of the dads in the area liked the grumpy and overly confident man, who lived alone there. Jake felt that no one would really argue with him. So, he accepted defeat and they stopped kicking the ball out in the street.

But something changed him yesterday. He woke up today with a deep anger in his young heart. He did not realize it at first, but as the day slowly passed by in the school, by the afternoon he was convinced that he has to pay Wilkins back somehow. He needs to feel the pain too. He needs to lose something he likes. Grownup or not, he had no right to deny playing in front of his house. The street does not belong to him! They did not cause him any harm. The ball merely touched the wheels of his car parked there, sometimes, and could not possibly break anything on it. And he could just hide it in the garage, anyhow, if he is so protective about his ride. He is evil, that's the only reason he is doing that. No one should listen to evil people. Evil people should be punished.

With his heart throbbing in his chest, he stalked close to the sport pickup, glanced around quickly, and up to the windows - the bluish flicker of a TV screen was seen inside. He quickly spilled the petrol all over the Cayenne, lit a cigarette from the secret stash of his brother, and set the car on fire.

He was shivering with excitement and satisfaction in his own bed, when the wail of the sirens approached the neighborhood. As he was listening to what's happening outside, he could not stop drawing that same geometric symbol in his small notebook, over and over again. With every try, he felt he was getting closer to the original - the one he saw flashing up in purple light, on the hand of the big black man.

<u>N</u>

Carrie slowly but surely started to panic.

Nick moved back into her parent's house a few days ago but still kept her apartment. She was heartbroken, could not stop crying for days. She always liked to be the center of attention, so Carrie was suspicious at first - but Mom was freaking out. They urged her to go to a doctor, but she refused. She wanted to be accepted, taken care of, but refused any sensible attempt at helping her. After a few days, Carrie got worried. Nick wasn't the same as before. It seemed she is drifting on a downward spiral towards total nervous breakdown, and they could do nothing to save her. She kept mumbling about the "one," inside, striving for control. At times, she seemed like she was hallucinating. When they asked what she sees, she never responded, just collapsed. Their parents decided it is time to bring her to get medical help, whether she wants it or not. They were ready to get her to safety against her own will.

And now, she was gone. Carrie screamed when she entered Nick's old room. A huge, crudely painted symbol covered almost full of the wall, the paint bucket and the brush thrown into a corner.

Carrie ran through the house, checked out every corner, every hiding place she could imagine, but she did not find her. After browsing through the open drawers, she has found a pack of meth crystals. She was crying like a baby, flames of guilt consuming her from the inside: her baby sister did drugs? Who barely even touched booze before? And now she is gone?

She was trying to control her breathing and gathering her strength to call 911 when she smelled something burning outside, in the backyard.

4

UNLEASHED

etrick sat in his car, holding his face in his hands. He had watched Amanda exit the coffee shop and carefully looking around the parking lot like a nervous deer. Her feet had moved briskly as she made it to her car, still scanning with wide eyes, and before Detrick could work up the nerve to do anything about it, she was driving away. Amanda was smart, perceptive, and beautiful, and he had sat there like a fool while she steered her car out of his life.

He gripped his hair in his hand and huffed bitterly. "Why did I have to make a deal out of it?" he asked himself. "Why? She didn't mean anything by it. She just wanted to talk is all, and I ran her off like I hated her. God!" he blared, pounding his fist on the dash. "What the hell is wrong with me?"

Angry and hurt, Detrick pulled a pen out of the cup holder with his right hand and held up his head with the left. The pen bounced and wiggled in his hand as the nervous tensions worked their way from his thrumming heart to the tips of his fingers. He jammed his eyes closed and ground his teeth against the sensation, furious with himself for blowing it. Chances were, he realized, he would never see that girl again.

Detrick rested his shaking hand against the center of the steer-ing wheel and snorted uncomfortably. He watched as the tip of the pen pressed to the spongy cover over the air bag and scratched a blue vertical line. His hand fell into his lap and Detrick stared at the mark for several moments. The blue seemed to glow on the light grey of the steering wheel, and Detrick experienced a calming effect to tracing the line with his eyes. The pen floated back up to the line and he began to draw without thinking, scratching hooks and curves and scribbling the lines until they stood dark and bold on the wheel. The form came into view; the only image he had created for days on end. Detrick followed the flow of the symbol with the tip of his finger and breathed deeply. His heart settled down to a normal beat and his head began to clear. He tossed the pen to his right and it popped against a pile of papers spread over the passenger seat. Lined pa-per. Copy paper. Pages from magazines. Dozens of scraps and pages were scattered over the seat and the floor of the car, and upon those pages the same symbol appeared thousands of times. Big. Small. The sized varied but the image never changed. The symbol made him feel good; it made him feel calm and safe.

"I want to feel like this," he whispered to the symbol on the wheel. "I want to feel like this forever."

A

"You've thought about this a lot, eh?" the older man behind the coun-ter said.

"I have," Amanda assured him. She smiled politely and laughed inside. 'Only if by a lot you mean all of this afternoon,' she thought giddily.

"And where do you want this put?" the man asked with a disinter-ested professionalism.

Amanda pulled up the sleeve of her shirt and touched her inner arm, a few inches above her wrist. "Here," she said with more confi-dence than she felt.

"Cool," the man said. "Travis will be out in a few minutes to get you all squared away."

Amanda thanked the man and moved to one side of the room. She had never been in a tattoo parlor, and the environment was a little intimidating. There were pictures all over the walls of tattoos, from the classic kinds she could picture on a sailor's arm, to paintings with incredible detail.

"Amanda?" a voice called from the counter. She looked to find a young man with a flat-billed baseball cap and thick reading glasses. He was wearing a thin white V-neck and a pair of burgundy chinos. Every inch of exposed skin from his jaw line down was covered in tattoos. The man must have been a peer of Amanda's, but she would never have imagined meeting him if not for today's adventure. "I'm Travis. You ready?"

Amanda nodded her head and followed the man to a small room with a padded table.

"So," Travis said in a friendly tone. "Why a tattoo?"

"Because I've always wanted one and now seems like a good time," she answered quickly while her eyes scanned the small space.

"Cool," he replied. "Cool. And what does this mean?" he asked, holding up the picture of the symbol. Amanda had taken a photocopy of the image and brought it in for a reference. "I know I've seen this before, but I can't remember where."

"It's from a novel I've been reading," Amanda explained. "This guy has this magic power to capture things in his book but he has to marry this woman he hates which is not surprising since she is a horrible person and he ends up... well..." Amanda looked into the disinterested eyes of the artist and bit her lips.

"It's just a good book, really," she said weakly. "And the symbol is kind of his thing. Why do you ask?"

"Honestly?" Travis asked with a peaked voice. "Because there are a ton of folks, mostly girls actually, that rush in here and get a symbol stamped on them. It's usually on a highly visible area, and often enough they grow to hate it. I'm trying to figure out if you really love this thing or if we should change the design up a little to make it easier to cover if you ever..."

"No!" Amanda barked sharply. She surprised herself with her tone, but that did not change the urgency she suddenly felt. The artist made a face and Amanda softened her own expression. "I mean no, please," she repeated in a more delicate manner. "It's perfect just like it is, and I promise that I won't ever grow tired of it."

"Your body," Travis replied.

"Great," she said politely, smiling warmly at the artist. "This is exactly what I want."

An hour later and Travis was leading Amanda to the front counter. "Keep it covered for the next couple of hours," he said, pointing at her arm. After that, just follow the directions on your instruction sheet." He handed a purple piece of paper to her that listed a bunch of do's and do not's with new tattoos. "Cool?"

"Absolutely," Amanda replied. "Thank you so much."

"I want to see you come back in here in a few weeks to show me what it looks like. 'Kay?" he said in a friendly tone.

"Sure," Amanda agreed, waving as Travis wandered down the hall and back to his parlor.

"That means he likes you," the man at the front counter shared.

"I'm sorry?" Amanda asked.

"Just sayin'," the man replied.

Amanda paid quickly, trying to hide her embarrassment. She thanked the man at the front counter and moved to the door. As she stepped outside, Amanda bumped into a customer on their way in. "I'm sorry," she gushed. "I didn't..."

"Amanda?"

She looked up and lost her breath. "Detrick?"

Detrick smiled sheepishly. "What are you doing here?"

"I just got a tattoo," She explained. "Like literally just now."

"Awesome." Detrick bobbed his head and made a face. "I can't let that happen again."

"What?" Amanda asked.

"I'm sorry for earlier when I left so quickly," he said. "It was rude and…"

"I was out of line," Amanda assured him. "I totally get it."

"So I would really like to see you again, though." He made a timid smile wiped a hand on his shirt. "So can I have your number? Maybe give you a text later and we can meet for another coffee and strange conversation?"

Amanda laughed and pulled out her phone. "What's your number?" He rattled it off and she texted him a quick note. "Now you have my number. Ball's in your court, Detrick."

"I'll see you later," he said, looking around them. "We can hang out in another doorway somewhere. It'll be great."

"I'm looking forward to it." Amanda moved past him and glided to her car, feeling amazing.

MO

With the stars over their heads and the grass under their bare feet, Orin and Michaela moved between the trees until they emerged on the top of a hill. The city was far below them, and the gulf was a black carpet beyond a still and quiet shore. Orin breathed deeply through his nose and his eyelids fluttered with chill in the air. The coolness filled his head and pressed against the walls of his lungs until he felt as though he was only moments away from flight. "The whole world," he said his eyes distant and wild. "The whole world is out there, waiting for us to do as we wish." He exhaled loudly and reached for Michaela's hand. He slipped his hand down her arm and threaded his fingers between her own. Michaela's hand did not respond. It hung there, lifeless and miserable. Orin leaned toward her and swung his attention to her expression.

Michaela looked over the hillside with a hopeless sensation in her stomach. "I have been so alone all my life," she confessed. "I have never had anyone. Not really, anyway. The world goes on around me, day after day. I watch it go by as though I was a tree planted next to a highway, allowed to live but forced to spend my life rooted to one place as everyone else passes me by." Orin gripped her hand and held it tightly in his. "I've always wanted a life of my own."

The gulf sang its endless song, and the world around them twinkled like the stars above them. "Every one of your dreams has just come true," he promised her. "There is nothing that is being kept from you. No one is standing in your way now. Every dream that you've ever had can be yours. And if anyone gets in your way, I will personally tear their throat from their neck."

She leaned her head upon his shoulder and squeezed Orin's hand in her own. "Promise?"

His tattoo emitted a soft purple glow from his hand, matching the color rising from her chest. "Promise," he replied quietly. "Promise."

<u>N</u>

"So just like this, huh?" the woman asked. Nicolette looked at the symbol on in the mirror, and gave a nod of approval. "Honey, I don't want to sound patronizing or anything, just, you know, with a tattoo of this size and exposure… it is our standard procedure to make absolutely sure about this."

Nicolette didn't have to think twice. "I understand," she said dreamily. Her tone was like a bride-to-be looking over her dream dress, or a teen getting their first car: euphoric. "This image means so much to me," she explained to the artist, "that if I could put it over my whole body in a pattern, I would."

"I can do that," the tattooist replied casually, mixing her ink.

"This will be fine, for now" Nicolette laughed, ecstatic with the position in which she found herself.

"This your first tat?" the woman asked, adjusting her tattoo machine.

"Yeah," Nicolette sighed, her eyes still locked on the image covering her whole face. The top of the symbol was nestled on her forehead, running down through her eyes, across her cheeks, meeting again at her chin.

"This will take most of the day. And it will take several sessions to finalize it," the artist checked. "And it is going to sting here," she said, pressing at the lines at the corner of the eyes, "and it will sting here," she added, touching her temple gently "I won't lie. It's gonna suck."

"That's fine," Nicolette assured her in a relaxed tone. "And I won't leave this chair until it is all done." Her words sounded like she was in a trance, and her eyes were focused on something beyond room.

"I'll start here," the artist said, pointing at the chin of Nicolette. "It'll hurt the least, and help you to prepare for the more sensitive parts."

"Don't worry about me," Nicolette sighed. "I'm fine."

The artist shrugged and dipped the needle into a small plastic well of black ink. "Hold still," she warned, and began to carve a thin and shallow line over Nicolette's face, splitting the skin with a thousand tiny pinpricks and filling the gap with dark ink. The buzz of the machine and the hum of the artist were all that could be heard, but Nicolette's mind was nowhere in the room.

As the artist marked away at her skin, Nicolette allowed her eyes to wander about the space. The studio was set up in a wide room faced with floor to ceiling windows, and decorated with waist-height dividers like short cubicle walls. Each little space had a black padded chair and a toolbox filled with tattoo supplied. Beyond the four booths, there was a waiting area and a front register. The back of the room had two doorways – one for supply and the other for tattoos that required more privacy.

At that moment, Nicolette couldn't understand why anyone would want to hide this experience from the world. She looked out the front windows at a downtown view full of cars, pedestrians, noise, and life. The sunlight shimmered off polished metal and glass, and people strolled by with determination on their faces and directions in their minds. Occasionally someone would wander up to the glass and pause to look inside and watch a tattoo come to life. Nicolette was toward the back of the room, but she could still clearly see every face that walked by. Some were worried and others were entertained. Some faces were offended, but some of those that stopped to look in seemed excited for her. One man nodded his head at her, but the next one looked heartbroken. 'So many people,' Nicolette thought, 'and so many feelings.'

Nicolette eyes floated back to the ceiling, and as she felt the ink-stained mess spreading over her face, she smiled. The power symbol was coming to life. It had been a savior; a redeemer; a light in the darkness. The man in the shadows had been there, haunting her every step for weeks.

But no longer.

The symbol appearing on her face will remain there forever, as a protector against the dark. The feeling Nicolette had for the simple line curving back over itself was more than love. She held a deep and personal reverence for it, the way a Christian looks on a cross or a Muslim looks at the star and crescent. The symbol wasn't the power itself, but the name of the force within her, and placing that name upon her skin was her way of giving herself to that power.

The one who saved her from darkness.

The one who gave her peace.

The one who rescued her.

As the buzzing of the tattoo machine held its steady pace, Nicolette looked around and smiled. She liked it there. With all the windows, there wasn't a dark shadow in sight.

In all her life, Nicolette couldn't remember a single moment where she felt as good as she did that evening. Every light seemed to shine a little brighter, and every bite of food was richer than it had ever been. Warmth seemed to radiate from her and the world was full of new perfumes, drifting about and making the world sweet and uplifting. Everything seemed possible to Nicolette and she moved through humanity knowing that she was safe; no longer could anyone touch her. The darkness fled from before her and in Nicolette's eyes, there were no more shadows. No longer could evil lurk in the darkness. The powers that had chased her for so long no longer held any power over her. Nicolette was free, and she loved every moment of it.

She entered her apartment and closed the door behind her. The sun was setting over the water and there was a burning glow that slipped along the carpeted floor right up to Nicolette's feet. She moved into the orange light and one step after the next she traced it to the bedroom. Bold and steady, Nicolette stared into her reflection in the window.

"You do not control me," she said to the reflection. "I am not afraid of you." Behind the shadow of her reflection, the tide rolled and crashed into the bay. "You wanted to take me," she said calmly, "but I am protected. I have a guardian stronger than you will ever be, and she has saved me." She leaned closer and pointed at the markings on her face. "Do you see?" she screamed at the glass. "Do you see? You tried to take me, but you failed. And now? Now you will never drag me away. I am free because of her; her seal is upon me."

The last sliver of the sun fell beneath the edge of the gulf and the world was alive with a soft, waning light.

"I am free," Nicolette announced to the reflection. "I serve only one."

Her hands hung at her sides, limp and clammy, in defiance of the energy she could feel surging through her veins. On her face, the new tattoo pulsed and hummed on her skin with such vigor that Nicolette could almost hear it. She closed her eyes and tipped her head back, thanking the spirit within her for its righteousness and its power to save. The ink shined with a soft purple glow and fresh red blood dripped down and ran through her face, like a dark tear. She smeared the blood on the bathroom mirror, watching the subtle purple glow of the huge tattoo on her face, shining in the dim light. She looked into the eye of her reflection for a few more minutes, and she was gone.

5

FALLEN

etrick let out a heavy, satisfied breath as he reached the top of the hill, and looked straight into the pink glow of the rising sun hovering low over the gulf. It was a beautiful, and quite early, spring morning. The morning air was brisk but the rays of sunlight already carried some pleasant warmth through. Detrick smiled and shifted his gaze towards the town below. His town.

Detrick took a deep breath, removed his polo shirt, and just stood there, enjoying the fresh drafts of wind on his skin. "It should feel this too..." he thought to himself "...I better let it breathe freely..." He slowly removed the foliage cover from his chest, and took of the bandage. His fresh, new tattoo still oozed out some black ink mixed with purple bloodstains but it did not feel sensitive at all. In fact, it felt perfect. Detrick looked at it for a few moments and he felt pride. Pride and responsibility. He felt privileged, to bear this sign over his heart, and felt a certain desire to forever qualify for it, to be worthy of it. He felt as a whole now. It was "only" a tattoo and yet, he felt the compelling and comforting dedication that only someone who willingly puts a permanent symbol on his own body can understand.

The tattoo felt "heavy," to his surprise. Instead of any itch or pain, it emanated a soothing, cold feeling, like the stainless steel of a broadsword. Or maybe a better description would be to compare it to the feeling of a breastplate. Protecting him and the ones he cares for, and declaring the values he is standing by, as a coat-of-arms. Hidden on his skin, but forever there. In the early morning sunlight, it almost seemed to radiate a faint, delightful purple glow.

Detrick looked down on the barely awake town and smiled. Something changed, that is for sure. He was filled with a sense of purpose, his doubts, and insecurities faded into a distant past, like it all happened eons ago. It is all over; a new, glorious chapter starts on this marvelous spring dawn. He does not need anyone, he is not depending on anyone, and he will simply do the right thing, as he always dreamed to do, not caring about what others say. His actions will speak for themselves. He finally accepted that he couldn't be eagerly looking for the approval of his so-called friends. He will not bend towards their every whim, what their petty and shortsighted minds come up with in the moment, locked in their small and insignificant lives. We are here to do more! A wave of enthusiasm washed over him. Why don't they understand this? Why did he himself not understand this earlier, so clearly, as a crystal lake hiding inside the crown of mountain peaks? He should have never been ashamed of wanting more from life, to experience moments of serenity and glory, like this one, and to always fight the good fight. With the symbol on his chest, he reached an important milestone. It seemed laughable, the shame he felt by his obsession towards this image - the way he has been drawing it for hours. It is so clear now, he wanted this change, and he was preparing for it. Deep inside, he nurtured these thoughts, while formulating the delightful curves and edges of the elaborate image. Now that he has become one with it, his new life just locked in place, with a satisfying bang.

No time to mess around. Just to enjoy life at its fullest, and walking the purest path. He watched the sparkles below, the reflections of the spring sunrise on the shop windows. He will be the good shepherd, if there is a herd worth guiding through the dark forest. He will tell Aaron to get his act together and set his relationship straight (literally), instead of ridiculing himself with the twisted favors he asks from the men he considers his best friends. And if he disagrees, he will face the consequences.

Suddenly he imagined the lithe body of Amanda, as she was hurrying through the parking lot the other day. He can thank so much to her, she does not have the faintest idea! She is so smart and her heart is in the right place. It is amazing though, how they both decided to have a tattoo on the very same day - on the same day they ever met for the first time. Fate has something in store for them, Detrick was convinced about that. Not sure what that is, but he hoped for the best, and he swore to protect her. A sudden burst of emotion blazed through his body, strangely, it started in his tattoo, filled his heart, raced around his arms, his legs and exploded in his brain in the end, picturing the girl who knows so much about books but so little about how to navigate the stormy seas of life. He will make sure she is always faring on safe waters. His grip locked around his phone in his pocket, his thumb drawing a small circle on the buttons, as if he was checking that all nine of them on the number pad were in place. He will call her. Right now, right here… if signal strength abides. He realized in awe, that his tattoo clearly looks like there is a purple hue around it now. Yet, he was not afraid for the slightest bit, and in all honesty, he failed to feel surprised. It seemed and felt like it is just as it should be.

He sighed and looked for a comfortable rock to sit down on. He got on his shirt, never minding the bandages - his tattoo is just fine, he can feel it. Tugging the plastic covering and the blood-and tint-soaked bandages in his pockets, he noticed a few cigarette stubs on the ground, with lively red lipstick markings on them. A few feet from the stubs, the rectangular shape of a bourbon bottle glinted in the early sunlight. Detrick snorted. Somebody clearly had a celebratory evening last night right here, where he came to contemplate and to take in the view. Showing not much respect for this beautiful spot with a commanding view on the town. His town. From this rock.

Detrick just sat there for a few minutes in complete silence and rejoice, watching the slowly awakening nature around him and the town below him, letting his mind roam freely, reviewing his plans for the future, about doing his dissertation, get some decent part-time job that he actually can put his heart in, spend more time with people who do matter and less with those who does not. Starting with Amanda. His stomach reminded him about the importance of a royal breakfast, so he quickly stood up, already thinking about how to phrase the breakfast invitation for her. He picked up the studs, put them inside the liquor bottle, and descended down on the trail, whistling a merry pop tune.

A

Amanda sat right in the center of her living room floor, surrounded by notes, drawings, open books, prints, her laptop, her tablet, candles, lampions, incense-burners. It was way past midnight, and time seemed to stand still and fly speedily like a group of sparrows, at once. All afternoon, she was practically gloating at her own beautiful new tattoo for an hour or so, taking a couple of dozen selfies wearing maybe less than decent outfits (and carefully saving them to an offline drive) and striking elaborately designed poses, in interesting illumination setups, applying filters, all the while not minding at all that her tattoo is basically throbbing on her forearm, still leaking some black and bloody moisture. Another couple of hours flew by as she organized and edited the photos, stopping sometimes, staring at an image where her tattoo seemed to come alive. She even put some of the pictures next to each other, while nervously checking the real tattoo as well, because sometimes it seemed that the pattern changed, expanded a bit, crawling up on her arm or down to reach her hands. It took some time to accept that it is just a game of shadows and after-effects. The notion of her tattoo coming alive was terrifying, but also exciting in a strange sense. It was also somewhat baffling that no matter how she tuned and tweaked the coloring of the pictures, it seemed on many of them (mostly on the best ones, the most beautiful shots) that the tattoo does not simply reflects light but it looked like it is emitting a faint purplish glow. It had to get dark outside for Amanda to realize that she had something totally different in mind for this afternoon. She snapped her laptop shut and dashed to her Celica to speed back to the Uni.

She used the last remaining opening hours of the library to gather as much info about the Rundaggers, the publishing company of her dear old book, and numerous other aspects of the story as she could. She was thriving: she had to admit she had the best time, like, ever. She always enjoyed doing research for the school assignments, putting together the pieces, ordering them in a structure, draw conclusions, but now she really has felt like doing something she was born to do. Her interest in her book got mixed with a sense of guilt though - she did not want to demystify the story, she was a bit afraid that uncovering too much about the story could lessen the enjoyment of reading it. She carefully designed the whole process: she wanted the get the symbol on herself, spend a few hours researching the book, and after that, with some candles and a glass (or two) of wine, getting to the end. She savored the moment when she will have to turn the last page and close the back cover on it, and tried to take the inescapable end as a small celebration. She wanted to know more about it. She wanted to get involved with it. She wanted to become part of it.

Amanda didn't have much to worry about spoiling the end for herself - the book had no digital footprint whatsoever, which was somewhat peculiar in itself. She uncovered some tiny bits about historical, geographical details, but nothing particularly revealing. She admitted that this project needs a much bigger library than this one. She hurried back home, prepared every note and device, and started processing through the last chapter as an elaborate ritual.

It was very much like dreaming awake. Amanda did not have much experience with drugs, but she guessed being high on psychedelics must feel like this - though she did not care and did not want to waste her thoughts on analyzing this, being afraid she might snap out of this delightful state of mind she had found herself in after a few hours. She was the reader and the author, creator and audience, a character inside the story and the one watching herself from the outside of it. She saw the image, the symbol on the pages of the book, on the screens, scribbled on the notepad, reflecting in the windows from the glow of her own tattoo, dancing around her in a delightful and terrifying waltz, getting closer, consuming her whole from the inside. She reveled in how Rundagger accomplished his goals and regained control in his life after all the tragedies he had to endure - his symbol was guiding him like a beacon of light. It all made sense; everything was finally put in its right place. Amanda did feel a certain remorse that she finished the book, but the ending made it apparent that there are other volumes; the story is continuing... she just needs to find it. She knew some people might consider this ridiculous but she felt without doubt that the book transformed her, changed her for the better. Now her geeky and book wormy nature seemed perfectly right, normal, she embraced and accepted her fate. Nothing will be the same after she got this marking on her body and although it was all peculiar to say the least, she simply could not worry about the strange symptoms and visions. She felt better, smarter even. She felt like the best of her has been brought out to the surface. Amanda looked around and felt connected to everything, the notes, the laptop, she had new insight, an inexplicable self-confidence, a bright light that leads her straight into an interesting and exciting future, shining in through the window, coming in from the... Sun? She lashed out to grab her phone to check the clock, and had to realize that it is actually 7 in the morning. The weight of the all-nighter she pulled without noticing it suddenly has fallen on her shoulders. She was exhausted, dizzy, and hungry like a wolf. But also there was some coy happiness inside her, and a great satisfaction, like she just accomplished something significant. Out of nowhere, Detrick came into her mind, a weird idea about she telling him everything she uncovered about the book, over a triple cappuccino and a load of chocolate cookies, then she sprang halfway up to the ceiling, letting out a small shriek, as the sound of her ringtone cut into the sleepy silence of her dim living room… with the name "Detrick" appearing on the screen of her phone in her hands.

MO

"What seems to be the problem, Officer…Delaney?" - breathed Michaela. She was arching through from the passenger seat, crawling halfway over Orin, one hand resting on his muscled thigh, the other clasping into the window of the pickup. Her sunglasses hovered at the edge of her tiny but pointed nose, as she looked up to the dark figure standing in the blazing sunlight.

"The problem, Miss, I'm very much afraid, is speeding. A quite… spectacular one, I must say "- answered Officer Delaney with a huge grin on his face. - "So I would kindly ask the gentleman driving the vehicle *again,* to get out of the vehicle, please, slowly, and put his hands on the roof. Now."

Michaela felt a slight tremor below her, as the muscle in Orin's thigh flexed. She spotted his hold strengthening on the steering as well, and the tattoo on his forehand flaring up with an angry purple. The police officer surely did not catch glimpse of that, but, he felt the tension growing in the bulky athlete below her sure enough.

"Aaaaaaall righty then, we will do just that, Officer Delaney!" snapped Michaela with cheerful irony, grabbed the door opener, and pushed out the door towards the slightly surprised policeman. She wiggled over her partner and crawled out of the huge black pickup at the driver's side with an unfazed look on her face. Her heels landed on the tarmac, one after the other, she pushed up her sunglasses, and threw a million dollar smile towards the policeman. His partner,

Officer Pierce, if Michaela got that right in the glaring sunlight, a sturdy redhead, stood a few yards away from them, her fingers circling over her sidearm like she was ready for a duel by the third ring of an imaginary bell. "Well this gon' be tricky." she thought to herself. She developed the habit of using a mockery of southern accent since she relieved that overly confident fellow of his truck, back at the park.

"ID, Miss. And I will require your partner to step out as well."

"Weellll…" Michaela let out, still playing with the faked southern country style, and a heavy waft of liquor with it "…there might be a small problem with that".

"Reveal your papers of identification, Miss, or else I will be forced to detain you."

"Oh, I know! I know. I just don't seem to be able to hold my concentration long enough to remember… where I put them… over the smell of… your most incredible… after shave." she gasped, each short sentence a little lower than the one before it, and bowing closer and closer to the chest of the officer. Delaney was listening intently; also leaning slightly closer to the young gal dressed in a revealing, black outfit, with a striking black tattoo in her cleavage, and froze after Michaela muttered the last words. She rolled her eyes under her green tinted black shades, as it all sounded way more stupid than she thought it will, but there was no time to come up with something wittier - and sweet talking males was never her forte anyway. It was enough, though: she lifted her right hand and touched Delaney's left arm, caressing down a few inches on it gently. The officer did not move an inch but Michaela knew from just that empty, disbelieving look on his face, felt it through the wave of a mystical empathic sense that it worked again, she has the opportunity, she just has to seize it. All or nothing. Bold and dangerous. Carpe diem. Gosh, she loved this new life of her, living on the bleeding edge.

She moved towards him with a graceful drift of her hip, and went on whispering hoarsely: "Listen, Officer, I need to tell you something… about the guy behind me in the car…please, I need you to know..." Delaney turned his head slowly as the girl moved her hands up his arms and his back, her forehead almost touching his chest, almost crying from desperation.

What on earth is she doing? And why doesn't he just command her to keep her distance? Pierce grinned like a cougar with all its muscles prepared for the deadly launch. She just could not believe her own eyes, as the suspect clearly established bodily contact with Delaney. She did not look armed but Pierce almost forgot to breathe by seeing this incredible breach of protocol, she had to forcibly stop herself from drawing her gun and plunging that disrespectful girls face down into the tarmac, taking the initiative from Delaney who supposed to be her superior.

Orin watched the policewoman in the mirror with a delightful grin on his face. He saw the symbols in the mirror, circling around her, in the bright springtime noon, and felt her utter helplessness. Made his day, and the next one, he felt. He almost wanted to draw a big sip from the bottle of whisky below his seat, just for the hell of it. But he rather shifted his dark gaze back to Michaela. He would really love to blast in the skulls of these clowns, but he did let the girl work them her way this time. It was a bright, peaceful joyride so far. Why ruin that laidback mood with a double homicide already?

"...He is... from a very problematic family, Officer... has such a hard time nowadays... we just came out to drive ourselves around a bit, you know, we mean no harm, we will be careful, I... promise" she breathed into Delaney's neck so close, that during the last words her nose touched the policeman's sweaty skin, with his veins throbbing below it as his heart pumped furiously. She then said something else, several things, or were only her lips moving, with no audible voice? However it was, Delaney slowly regained his composure. He flashed his eyes towards his battle-ready partner, took a step back, and mumbled something about driving safely and responsibly. And walked back to his cruiser with long, heavy footsteps, nodding shortly at the astonished Pierce.

The wheels of the truck spurted waves of dirt and left the patrol there in a cloud of dust, engine rpm quickly reaching dimensions of dubious legality.

N

"I brought you… I brought you raspberry candies!" Nicolette shone a royal smile over the sniveling face and took the small package from the twitching hands. She gently caressed the unshaven cheek of the strung out kid, who bathed in the imaginary golden radiance he felt and saw reaching out towards him, from the girl's heart, in lush, warm waves of love.

She was lying on the worn sofa, resting her face on her arm, with a growing pile of drying pizza, cheap wine, chocolate bars, beer cans, and a plethora of psychedelics in front of her, on the dirty carpet. She always ended up sharing the offerings of her new friends with them, which they always took with utmost gratitude.

Six guys and two girls lay around in the filthy center room of the hundred year-old abandoned house in the swamped outskirts of the city. City council deemed the old plantation mansion inhabitable, dangerously close to collapsing - but no one bothered to chase the squatter junkies away. This was not the part of town where the authorities had the time or inclination to do so.

Nicolette could not exactly piece together how she got here if she even wanted to try. But she rarely cared. Everyone here was so kind to her. It took her a few days to figure out why they like her so much.

The lost and the forgotten gathered in this creepy old house to shoot whatever psychoactive substance they could get their hands on. Speedballers, meth heads, H-addicts all appeared here, but every single one of them dropped pills or put tiny pieces of paper on their tongues or below their eyelids to chase the dragons of the worlds beyond the veil of matter as well. They looked like a ragtag gang of sorts, ordered within an unfathomable system of seniority, locality, and bloodlines, with their own twisted strategy for survival and getting high while doing so. She was shivering in a dark corner at first, merely tolerated, after it became evident that she is not police, means no harm, and is utterly broke. Her awe-inspiring facial tattoo drew some attention but also kept the gang at bay. She was about to go and get some food, anyhow she can, when Jason crawled over to her, and babbled about the beauty of her face - meaning the elaborate symbol carved on it, without a doubt. The boy went on, high as a clock tower, for ten minutes straight, and then he passed out. When he came to, he never wanted to leave Nicolette, "The Priestess" alone again, and made sure she is treated well. That made some more people curious. And the more of them got close to her, the more stayed, tears in their eyes, growling in ecstasy and serenity. They thought of her as their savior, a glorious angel bringing light into the darkness they spent their miserable days before her arrival. Later even more of them came, skeptical, doubtful, and all of them, after some time, realized that what the others say is true.

The junkies had the best trips ever, with Nicolette around. They dreamt awaken about sunny fields, flying through rainbows in vast open skies, diamond stars, and peaceful celebrations. They had a good time together. They started to trust each other more, opened their heart and shared the love. Nicolette found herself bringing a hippy heaven to life, descended down right from the lucid dreams and imaginations hailing from the beaches of Goa, and from the planks the stages of Woodstock were assembled from.

They loved her the most, and admired her Symbol. The secret, ancient markings on her face, which appeared in their hallucinations again and again, standing still, floating, emitting light or moving in elaborate patterns, reaching out from Nicolette's face towards them, hugging them, covering them and protecting them for good, for now, and forever.

Nicolette never knew scarcity, hardship, or distress again - she got what always belonged to her. She gave them peace of mind, told them that everything is going to be all right from now. She gave them the kindest visions she was capable of bringing up, benevolently veiling the misery, the stench, and the hopelessness they were all groveling in.

6

PROTOCOL BREACH

D

"I could hardly tell the difference. Reading it or imagining it or living it… it became sort of the same." - said Amanda, wolfing down another pile of chocolate cookies.

Detrick stared out the window, listening intently, but also buried under his own thoughts. At least, it looked that way. In reality, on the background created by the small park outside the coffee shop, he saw his own reflection on the window. The reflection also reflected back some of the sunlight coming in from the glass door entry, which created a playful golden halo over the head of his own reflection. As the door opened and close, the light flickered and danced. He saw something like his own symbol there, which somehow just out of innocent randomness, emerged from the flickering reflections.

"What is happening with us?" he asked, quickly turning back to his breakfast partner. The bite stopped in Amanda's mouth, as she looked back from her hunched pose. The mouthful of cookies slowly wandered across into her left cheek, then back into her right, as she looked inquisitively at the guy sitting across the table. His eyes were glinting icy blue; a shudder stern layer appeared below his regular, soft voice.

"And please, don't you ask, what do I mean." he added.

Amanda gulped, and swallowed slowly, as it was exactly what she wanted to ask. She understood Detrick's request perfectly though. She wanted to ask what he means for two reasons: first, to make sure he's really talking about their special... *condition*, and second, to buy some time. For she did not have the faintest idea what to answer to that question, although totally accepted its validity.

"You spent the whole night with basically starting up a monograph about that book. You must have drafted some theories at least."

Amanda sighed and put down her cup. "Okay. Well. Honestly: not much."

"We know that there's this guy who can basically lock stuff into his drawings. Including people. He gets into trouble all the time, no one understands him..." her eyes wandered off from Detrick to gather her thoughts and she looked outside to the park. Amanda imagined Rundagger sitting on one of the benches; doing a sketch about a flower, or maybe a bird... she got touched by the memory. Finishing the book did not sever her connection to the tragic lead character at all.

"...but anyway, he is kind of redeemed by the symbol in the end."

"Oh yes, the symbol." nodded Detrick. He was somehow distant. And certainly not amused.

"Yeah, I mean, there is not really a way back for him to his old life or anything, but... at least he can start anew and accept what is happening around him." - added Amanda with a timid smile.

"Really?" - smiled Detrick with a quizzical look on his face. "Amanda, tell me, isn't this whole narrative a little familiar to you?"

"Wha..." Amanda wanted to ask, "What do you mean?" again, but she bit into her thin lip instead. She felt that Detrick would deem that inappropriate, just like last time. She fell silent and cast down her eyes and thought to herself. What is this guy's problem? And why does she feel that actually this time he has a point? Sure enough, he is being fully assertive - she did not have any reason to feel offended. Wherever he is going, it is something remarkable. Amanda felt like

Detrick, with his straightforward questions, is leading her to a secret clearing in a dark forest, a place she also knows about… she would have just avoided going there for a little longer. Like, until visiting it becomes absolutely necessary.

"Of course, you don't know it yet…" he said. "Let's take a walk. The weather is so nice. I'll take care of the bill." - He said quickly, and did so. Amanda admittedly liked this guy from the time they bumped into each other, but today he was somewhat different. Still nice, still gentle, still funny, still seemed a bit lost… but today he was somehow more confident. Of course, she barely knows him already; still it felt like something changed. And admittedly - she couldn't help but liked this changed Detrick even more.

Detrick didn't say a single word for a while, and Amanda didn't feel like breaking the silence. He led her to a bench in a peaceful corner of the park, under two young cherry trees. "Okay. Take a look at this." and removed his shirt with a single powerful yank. Amanda's mouth fell open, and closed, and opened again. And closed.

"I… that… Wow." She nodded, blushed, and removed a stubborn curl from her eyes again and again. She glanced away from Detrick's tattoo and glanced back. She also had to take a mental note about how his upper body looks way more well-sculpted than she had thought - a certain *nobility* radiated from it, Amanda almost chuckled over how silly that sounded. The situation got so embarrassing that she had no idea what to do at this point. Thankfully, Detrick slowly took up his shirt again, took a deep breath, and turned towards the center of the park, sitting next to the girl. Amanda held her bag on her lap with both hands, her fingers felt through the soft matter to remain in contact with the stiff spine of the hardcover book inside it. Although she finished it last night, it felt like a good idea to keep it close to her. Detrick slowly started talking.

"We met for the first time in that coffee shop. And only hours later, we meet again, right in a doorway again, only this time it's a tattooing place. We go there to put a symbol on ourselves, for the rest of our lives. Yeah, as you can see, I wasn't there to check out the interior, or to meet bikers either. I went there to ask for a tattoo, my design strictly... which apparently looks almost the same as yours."

"Yeah. Weird. In fact, it looks like they complete each other, you know what I mean? Like, they could be attached at the end."

Detrick nodded. Amanda wandered about the stern look on his face. He is taking it all so seriously. And yet, he might be right about that. Where is this all going?

"So you read about this guy who can do magic, by drawing stuff. He gets into trouble, gets saved by the symbol, and off he is to new adventures. And we? We get obsessed by this symbol..."

"Yeah, well, you know me... I like books! For me it's no big deal to get a little hooked on a certain book..."

"...with the lamest story ever? Give me a break. I know you are a smart girl, I know you read a lot, I mean, no, I don't *really* know you, but it just figures, okay? So, you've probably already read most of the best pieces that the history of literature can offer. And you tell me that the adventures and mishaps of Mr. Rundagger is *so* captivating that you're pulling an all-nighter and just google every factual information from it to extend the reading a little longer? A guy drawing stuff into his notebook that disappears? Seriously? I mean, it can be awesomely written, I did not read it. But I'm sure Poe could have drafted a more engaging plot before he finished his cup of tea, on any given rainy afternoon. So, what did you just tell me, did you miss a whole day of lectures at the Uni, just to stay with this amazing piece of romantic fiction?" "Yyyyip. Two of them, actually."

"Okay. Fine. Does this kind of thing happen regularly in your life, Miss?"

"Nnnno. Like, it never happened before, actually. I can confirm that, Mister. But that is a really good book!"

"Amanda. This is the best day of my life so far."

The girl gulped, and a quick "What-do-you-mean?" sprang from her lips before she could stop it. She turned red like a traffic light.

"Yeah, and I'm not just saying this because I have this delightful opportunity to share this sunny morning with you. It literally is the best day of my life. The best I've ever felt. Ever. And I'm not even feeling bad about saying this out loud; I know it sounds like I'm tripping. But I just don't care. Because this is the complete truth. And because, deep down, I'm totally convinced that I don't have to play and pretend before you, no harm will ever come by me being honest with you. And, most of all, because I know you feel the same."

Detrick inserted a slightly dramatic pose, and ended his speech with a recurring motif:

"What the HECK is happening with us?"

"This is how checkmate must feel like for the King." Amanda thought to herself, but said nothing, just laid back on the bench, stretched and crossed her sneaker clad feet, took a deep breath and let everything unfold whatever fate has in store for her from now on.

A long silence descended upon them. Only the birds chirped, and distant traffic sounds echoed through the spring morning. An old lady walked her dog in front of them, crossing their field of vision. She smiled as she passed the student couple sitting there in a contemplative silence.

"Do you believe in the supernatural?" it was again Detrick who broke the silence. He really had no intention to corner the girl. But he simply was convinced that they need to get to the bottom of whatever is happening with them, and they need to do it sooner rather than later. And he knew that without Amanda, he has no chance to dig deep. She holds the key, he was sure about that. It must be something to do with that book.

Amanda let out a big breath. She was happy that this conversation meandered back to a territory that at first seemed more homely and safe for her.

"Well, you can't *believe* in the supernatural. It is basically how you view the world. If you prefer the materialistic narrative, and you encounter, let's say, a purple dragon flying through the sky, you look for a scientific explanation. If you fail to find one, you leave the question open. You still won't believe that you saw an actual dragon actually flying through the sky - there must be a scientific explanation, you just don't have it is all. Whereas if you think that magic, or dragons, are real, it is no longer supernatural for you. It is just the way everything is."

Detrick grinned. "That's gonna be an A plus for Miss Pace, thank you for your wonderful epistemology coursework presentation, now everyone please open your textbooks, we will follow on with the postmodern critique of Nietzsche's Thus Spoke Zarathustra"

Amanda bit on her tongue and let out a tiny giggle. She wasn't happy about how Detrick reacted to her - slightly divertive - move, but she was a bit flattered by the guy even knowing the word "epistemology". Arts were not an inherent area of his studies. He did have some reserves!

"Look," he turned to face her again, with that stern look on his face again. "I understand, okay? I get it. You feel it. You know it just as well as I do. And no matter how deep you go into it, it just gets more complicated, right? Now I understand what you meant about how you felt last night, when you read the ending. It feels revealing, but it is anything but revealing. When you focus on the details, they drift away. Don't worry about it. Don't worry about anything, Amanda. We will get through this, we will get to the end. I promise you. All I want to say that I'm here for you, with you, and I promise I will protect you, no matter what, and we will make the most of this. So... just nod a tiny bit, if you agree. If you're with me."

Amanda gulped and nodded a tiny bit. She was relieved and happy. Detrick got it. He got her. So there is a living being with an XY chromosome setting that seems to understand and accept her - just in the time when she seems to need it most. She could not say a single word, but felt grateful. She was considering forcing a smile to appear on her tightly closed lips, but Detrick got up quickly.

"Gimme a sec." he told her "I just can't watch this, I need to check them out. It will take only a minute."

A

Amanda followed his determined footsteps with her eyes and she realized Detrick is approaching a group of kids in their early teens, or younger. Hard to say with today's kids. Her eyes widened - they played with a soccer ball, but the game seemed to shape up a little unfair for one peculiar kid, standing in the center of their loose circle. All of the others were kicking the ball, quite forcefully, to hit him. They passed the ball around to give each other another opportunity for hitting the guy who had to defend his face or stomach with his hands - when they shouted at him and called him a cheat. When the lonely guy tackled them, and got the ball, they brutally pushed him away by shouldering him. If he fell, they did not stop and kicked him with the ball from point blank range. It all escalated right in front of her... the kid seemed to retreat into full defense, curled up on the ground, when Detrick got there.

She watched the scene intently. They were too far for her to hear them, so it was like watching an old silent movie. One of the kids just took a few running steps to gather his momentum for a decisive kick into the ball, that would send the truncated icosahedron, pumped hard and made of leather, into the ribs of the kid who found himself at the lower end of group dynamics today. The attackers shooting feet literally stopped in the air as he was called by Detrick - Amanda just craved for knowing what he said. The boys seemed to turn into a statue group depicting the ferocity of youth. Detrick did not raise his voice. By the looks of his body language, he asked rhetoric questions, told short and powerful sentences, like a parable, and the boys just stood there, sometimes nodding, slowly gathering around him in a semi-circle, and suddenly, as Amanda watched in awe, two of the kids casually stepped over to their earlier prey and helped him to his feet, while grouping around Detrick. They were listening; some of them said something, answering to the young adult in their company. They all seemed to agree about something. Then, Detrick raised his hand high and for the first time, let out his voice a bit. Amanda only picked up the ending and concluded that the sentence probably went like this:

"Then do something about it!" - and the kids just blasted away from him, shouting in bold satisfaction and agreement, reaching full speed and passing the ball in elaborate moves, as they crossed the park and disappeared behind the bushes. The loud kicks on the leather ball were audible for minutes, as they chased it down the road, running further down the hillside.

Detrick returned with a smug look. "What did you tell them? It was awesome!" - asked the girl, barely being able to hold back her curiosity.

"Nah, nothing really, just asked them some questions, they got to the conclusions themselves. They just figured out a better way to spend this Saturday morning than kicking one of them to death. That's kind of boring anyway, isn't it?"

"Never seen something like that before. You do have a way with kids."

"I dunno, really, I just had to tell them what I had in my heart, on my mind, I usually feel awkward around kids. I did so now, too. You know, I can't stand bullying. Actually, I feel sorry for them. The bullies." he added with a smug smile "They must have so much pain inside them. All that pain, burning you from the inside. Let's move." he said and reached out to help Amanda up. They strolled through the park, enjoying the carefree, mellow mood. They both enjoyed the fact that they tried to talk things through, failed at it, and it still just convinced them. No matter what, they will help each other through this. Amanda was giggling, staring at her phone.

"What's that? Funny tweet?" asked Detrick.

A tiny smile was drifting back and forth on Amanda's expressions. After a few seconds of consideration, she passed her phone. Detrick casually looked at it, then froze right there and slowly took the phone into his hands, carefully, as if he was handling an explosive device.

"Hhh…how?" - was all he managed to word. On the screen, there was a photo. It was a young couple in a park, walking on a gravel trail - it was them, from a slightly elevated and tilted angle. Sunrays and reflections burned through the image, adding some beautiful lens flare effect and subtle glow. Right between them, in a second story window of the office building far behind, the reflections formed a geometric pattern. Detrick wasn't even surprised to find it somewhat similar to their tattoo patterns.

Amanda only smiled under her tiny nose, winked with one eye, and turned her head in a certain direction. Detrick followed the movement. He saw a lamp pole - with a CCTV security cam resting on it, pointed exactly to their direction.

"Well, wow. How did you get access to it?"

Amanda shrugged and put the phone back in the pocket of her hoodie. "I didn't. I just asked it to do it. Or to be exact, I asked my phone to ask her to do the shot and relay back the image to me."

"Soooo, the CCTV system is female, right?"

Amanda smiled and shrugged again. "All elaborate systems feel like that, yeah." She grabbed the local daily tabloid newspaper from the bench they were passing, to hide her blush, and to satisfy her constant longing after the information flow. She flipped the page.

"Holy smokes. There's three of us now," - she snapped, and curled up on the bench instantly. Detrick sat next to her to take a look, with a sudden surge of energy.

Page two featured a report about a local crime story. A girl went missing, but before leaving for good, she broke all the mirrors in the house she lived in with her parents and older sister, and built a fire from all the dolls the girls have been playing with when they were kids. The dolls had their bellies carved open and their eyes torn out, before badly burnt.

"Well that is creepy, to say the least."

They quickly scanned the contents of the article, and returned for the quarter-page photo next to it. Over the faded photo from the ID card of the girl, there was an image from the scene, which looked to be an upstairs room, probably the girls'. The wall across the door was almost fully painted in a dark color with a crude brush. It was a symbol, very much like the one Detrick and Amanda tattooed on themselves yesterday. According to the caption, the brush was found in the room with the missing girls fingerprints on it.

Her name was Nicolette Jennings.

<u>M</u>

Michaela watched in awe, as the flames consumed the pickup they've been using so far. She did not mind the change however. The truck was convenient and comfy, but it constantly reminded her of its previous owner, that full-of-himself redneck she sent out cruising into the nearby park after he hit on her. The red hood of the Mustang under her bottom felt like a very natural choice. Suited the color of her fingernails, too.

The driver Orin looked out through the side window (with the window closed and the seatbelt fastened) probably had a different opinion about all what transpired, or rather, he would have, had he remembered anything about it. Michaela kissed the shivering guy goodbye to make sure he has only pleasant, and more importantly, incredibly vague memories about the grand theft auto he has fallen the victim of. "Dressed in black, looking badass" figured as a very fitting and conveniently unusable description to share with the authorities, when they eventually get to question the guy.

Orin finished packing - or rather, simply throwing in the loot to the backseat of their new muscle car. Liquor, sweets, cigarettes, soda - nothing on which a human being could survive upon, but still, they never seemed to run out of energy. They barely even slept since they left town, just chilled out for a couple of hours when they have found an appropriate stop. The hulking figure joined her sitting on the hood of the car, putting a black cape, part of a cheap leftover Halloween dress they found at the shop they robbed, on her shoulders - a deed of chivalry, which seemed a bit unnecessary as the evening wasn't so cold yet.

They watched the truck spewing flames, as more and more flammable material inside its huge metal body reached the heat levels necessary for combustion. Orin casually hugged the girl, who almost disappeared in his low shadow cast by the setting sun. Michaela held herself for a while, then slowly gave in, and rested her head on Orin's shoulder. The tattoo on her chest let out a subtle glow, mirroring the evening sunlight, as she half-heartedly channeled some of her power into their touch. She played a delicate balancing game with Orin, which ultimately, she had to admit, will not suffice. She did not want to seduce him - quite the opposite. Orin clearly expressed his liking towards her, and his frustration slowly grew, as the girl seemed to ignore his feelings. Michaela tried to "tame" him, but her power wasn't so simple and straightforward in his case. He, in the end, was also *different.* Just like her. There was a subtle feedback when she used her power on him, but it was way tuned down compared to a regular human being. She was also afraid that he might feel her machinations and would be angered by them. And of course, he wasn't that stupid. He knew all too well what effect she has over men. Through her own powers, she tried to express that she needs his company, just not *that* way. She wanted to enhance the protective feelings of her new partner in crime, and dampen down the physical attraction - problem was, it was almost impossible to separate the two. Michaela, deep inside her, begged for the understanding of Orin, but knew for good that in the long run, her strategy is futile. She bitterly admitted to herself that eventually she would have to let the footballer have a go at her, if she wants to keep him company. She loathed even the thought of it - *any* man having power over her, getting intimate with her felt like a huge slap in the face. She felt so strong when she acquired this new life, the tattoo gave her a fresh start with huge possibilities. And here she is again. Life is somewhat bleak. There is no one out there now, just her, and him. Michaela watched the slow fire dancing in the engine compartment under the open hood of the pickup truck, as it was releasing thick, black smoke towards the starry evening sky. She felt she just wanted to see all the world burn with it.

O

"Orin Campbell, African-American, well built. Has been charged with assault, battery, charges have been dropped. Got into a street fight, nothing serious. College student, football player. No serious illness in medical records, lower-middle class family with no crime history. Part-time jobs, his employers describe him as dependable, if not overly enthusiastic. I know him, always seemed like a cool kid, an average guy who tries to get by."

Officer Fitzpatrick sighed, and attached a photo next to the criminal file on the whiteboard. It was showing Orin with his two fists raised, the tattoo on his left forehand glowing in a purple light. "That is no technical glitch or somethin'. Several testimonies confirm that the tattoo was sort of... glowing. That's new for me; I'm waiting on the report if that is some kinda electronic paint."

"Highly unlikely." answered Agent Moss. A quick shade of frustration ran through her face, and then she blew a bubble from her gum and let it explode. She looked bored as hell, but nodded towards the sheriff, signaling that he should continue.

"So, yeah, I think you know all the rest." the round, brown, slightly egg-like figure of Fitzpatrick turned back towards the board. "Left the hospital, and from there, we had only presumptions about his whereabouts and possible connections to several crimes committed in the county in the last 48 hours, until... you, ma'am, showed up."

"Lisa. You can either call me Lisa, or Agent Moss, if you prefer. Drop the ma'am," said the woman in the dark dress, and added after a slight pause: "Please. And do continue. I'm all ears."

Fitzpatrick looked at the board, back to the agent, down to the papers, on the board again and back to the agent again. He let out a small sigh. Why does this have to feel *exactly* like a verbal test did, back at high school?

"Oooookie-doke. Well. He supposedly left town in a black Ram with Michaela…"

"…Kaminski?" - followed up Agent Moss, glancing at the papers in front of her.

"Yip. Yes, ma'… Lisa. Uhm, Miss Moss, *Agent*… Moss. Certainly."

"Yeah, skip the descriptions, I got them, her ID is solid. Multiple witnesses at the restaurant, security cam, confirmed by relatives and roommates. Also a student. No proven contact with Campbell before, right?"

"That is right. Agent Moss. Righty."

"Officer, let me ask you this, without, you know, any push or something, just out of sheer curiosity…"

The sheriff felt a cold droplet of sweat slowly rolling down on his temple. "Yes, certainly, yes?"

"Why didn't you put out an APB on the vehicle they robbed from the parking lot in the same day the guy died and miraculously returned to life and walked out from the hospital with his shiny UV tattoo in full blaze?"

"Well, uhm, the owner did not report it in. And he neither pressed charges ever since."

"No wonder, since he is high as a mountain on sedatives. After he was picked up from the park nearby, unconscious, robbed, and quite possibly, raped."

"That, uhm, we don't know that yet for sure."

"Oh yeah! Sure. Sorry for running ahead. He was just found lying face down, within the bushes, with his jeans cut open with a crude cutting object, from behind."

"That is correct. We did find a connection with the juvenile arson case though. Jake Jordan. In his testimony, he says he has met someone with a glowing tattoo, in a park, on the day before. A tall, athletic African American."

Agent Moss put a black pin into the map on the wall, right into the hospital, one into the park, and another one to the restaurant. Than another one, at the westward road, roughly seven miles out of town.

"How about Delaney?"

"Officer Delaney? Uhmm, he is suspended, Agent Moss."

"Uhumm. His wife reported…" she leaned back at her table, weighing on her two palms, browsing through the documents, then she looked straight at the sheriff over her black sunglasses with a wicked grin "… sexual assault."

"I… I don't even know where you get this information from, everything is under investi…"

"Poor, poor woman. You know, she must have been *really* freaked out if she reported something like this in, right when it happened."

"Delaney is in custody, we are taking his testimony. Due process underway, Agent Moss." said Fitzpatrick. His mouth curled down on both ends like he turned into a bulky catfish miraculously appearing out in the dry.

"It did not require the greatest logistic efforts to lock him up, since he was already answering your questions when his wife called. Because his partner filed official complaints about how he handled a pullover situation earlier that day."

"This has nothing to do with…"

"It was. A. Black. Dodge. Ram. It has *everything* to do with our Bonnie and Clyde."

"Agent Moss…" the sheriff cleared her throat, touched her fingers together nervously "… with all due respect, the owner of the vehicle did not file official complaints. Delaney has an impeccable record. He is a great officer, a good man, he loves his family, and he was on his way to become the next sheriff of this town. I'm certainly hoping he still is. We are helping out in whatever family troubles he got himself into, and the breach of protocol investigation is underway, based on the report of Jacqueline Pierce. The hospital did not call in any emergency. Jake did not mention Campbell helping him in the arson, or even talking about setting his neighbor's car on fire. Miss Kaminski was behaving normally, apart from getting assistance from the restaurant staff because she seemed ill, before walking out, and probably leaving together with Mr. Campbell in Mr. Roderick's vehicle. We were in the process of analyzing these strangest of occurrences, right until you showed up. I'm... here to assist you, Agent Moss, and I'm positive we did everything by the book. If you have anything that can help us solve these issues, if you know anything about what the hell is going on with Kaminski and Campbell, please, address."

Moss exploded another gumball and smiled at the sheriff wickedly. She certainly started to like this Fitzpatrick character. She started to consider how to get him up to speed with maintaining the required confidentiality, when the sheriff's cell rang. He got it up and listened into it for a good half a minute, with a look on his face that almost made Moss giggle. She spun herself around in the office chair, seemingly to look out on the window, but in fact more to hide her inappropriate cheer. Fitzpatrick voice sounded hoarse when he answered to the call finally:

"So what on earth does he mean by saying 'superpowers'?"

N

Nicolette was sitting atop a throne of thrash, raised by her strange cult for her, in a dark alley, at night, when they ruled the streets nearby. Her followers sat before her, around an oil barrel fire. The walls in the alley were painted with the symbol, the symbol from the visions and dreams of her people, the symbol covering her full face. The drawings were small scratches and elaborate graffiti, numerous in shapes and sizes, as the junkies came and recreated the symbol in a religious ecstasy. They listened to her intently, as she spoke, her hands reaching out, and tears filtered from their eyes as beautiful butterflies made of heavenly lights flied out from her upward held palms. She wore golden necklaces and bracelets over her tattered and torn grungy outfit: gifts from her followers that they robbed in the area. The police locked several of them away as they grew increasingly reckless, but new ones came on every day. Although almost all of them were heavily addicted to illegal substances, now even clear ones, bums, alcoholics, lost kids, street thugs joined them just to enjoy the peaceful company and the unearthly radiance of The Priestess, as they called Nicolette. After a while, all of them became obsessed by her - and her symbol.

Detrick bit on his lip as he cautiously walked in the alley, cornering around the bodies (sleeping? passed out? or even dead?) that lied there in the filth, in the dark, grabbing Amanda by her wrist and leading her, defending her with his body.

A single day was enough for them to locate the missing girl, only by following her trail. After picking up the newspaper on the bench, they drove to the neighborhood. Since they knew her full name, and they had a rough description of the house from the photo in the newspaper and the text of the article, online maps and certain databases helped them pinpoint her family address quickly. Under Amanda's fingers, every digital device sang exactly what they wanted to hear.

Arriving at Nicolette's house, it was Detrick's time though. He moved forward and presented their case with a natural elegance. The parents were heartbroken and understandably reclusive; they have had enough of the all too revealing press coverage, the waves of neighbors and relatives hurrying to their need but in reality, only hindering the progress they could offer to the authorities, and making it harder for them to come to terms with their fears.

Somehow, they have found relief in the open hearted and calm approach of Detrick, his genuine helpfulness. In the end it was Nicolette's sister, Carrie, who told them about the drugs they have found in Nick's room. Luckily, the press did not get a hint about that.

Detrick made some phone calls and they easily got to the dealer. The police questioned him already and he had no clue at all - Nicolette probably got to his stuff through one of his clients. But then, he noticed the elaborate pattern tattooed on Amanda's forearm.

"Yo, are you guys like one of her 'followers', too?" He tells them about "The Priestess" he saw lately, the queen of all the junkies in the suburbs, who makes any trip hundred times better, and who has an insane web like tattoo all over her face. When they showed him the photo of Nicolette, he nodded. That is The Priestess.

"Detrick... these people... I mean shouldn't we call 911? I can't tell if they are dead or not..." whispered Amanda, staying as close to Detrick as she was only a small, shivering shadow of the man walking closer to the end of the alley.

"You came to show the Priestess your appreciation? BOW in her presence!" hissed a guy at them, coming closer to them from the shadows encircling the flickering fire of the oil barrel. He was wielding a rusty machete, with a trashcan lid hanging in his left like a shield - he looked like a macabre mockery of a medieval guard, complete with an iron fireplug cap on his head.

While Detrick explained that they are indeed here to see the girl he is referring to, Amanda became overwhelmed with the number, coloring, and size of the symbols all around them on the walls. She heard the markings whisper about the numerous mental conditions and terrifying drugged up visions their creators went through, while putting them up on the wall.

"Let them come through!" a gentle voice tingled towards them from the depths of the alley. The figures sitting around the barrel rose, as a young woman came ahead from the shadows behind it. "I've been expecting these visitors. Please come and join us!"

It was Nicolette, with her terrifying face tattoo glinting in harmony with the lights of the fire.

"My lady" Detrick stated, and to a sudden inspiration, he half-kneeled before the smiling girl coming forward. "We have heard much about you. We are sure you are one of us, and now I will show you what I speak is truth."

The small group murmured in surprise as Detrick unbuttoned his shirt, pulled the light fabric apart to reveal his tattoo on his chest, glowing now in a similar light, just as Nicolette's. Amanda looked at Detrick in amazement, while glancing around nervously. After a short hesitation, she also turned her forearm out, letting everyone see her tattoo clearly as well.

"Oh yes, you are serving the One as well! I've had dreams about you and couldn't wait for you to show up!" shouted Nicolette happily. She ran towards the puzzled Detrick and hugged him hard.

"My friends, my brothers and sisters, dwellers of this sad, shadowy reflection of the world of true and eternal light! I will join these people now, to bring forever harmony and peace to you all, and everyone who has the eyes to see it, the ears to hear it, the heart to take it in! *Rejoice!*" - she shouted, pushing both her arms in the air, and a bright bubble of sunlight exploded from inside her, chasing everyone around her into an ecstatic, mesmerized bliss. Nicolette stepped between the unaffected, but certainly confused new guests, grabbed both of them by the arms and urged them out to the entry of the alley.

"C'mon, c'mon, sweethearts" she murmured with a faint smile "Let's move out before they come to!"

7

BROKEN CODE

<u>D</u>

etrick sank into one of the comfortable armchairs in the hall of the city library. He watched Amanda's slightly hunched back as she did her magic in front of the public computer screen, with half a dozen open books spread around the keyboard in a semi-circle.

He took this short pause with a reserved pleasure, the first one since they left the park together. He contemplated on all that transpired since, especially last night.

Soon after they snatched Nicolette from her throne, they steered Amanda's Celica in front of probably the most glamorous hotel in the city. The Priestess needed a hot bath and a good night's rest, that was clear as daylight, but Detrick simply could not find any acceptable explanation about why on earth he instructed Amanda to drive there - like it was second nature. An axiom. We need a place to stay? Let's go to a 5 star hotel! Why, *where else* should we go? No one argued. The girls just let him decide. The shivers went up his spine as he tried to piece back, again and again, the line of thinking, and failed at each attempt. There was *no* line of thinking. He did not know what seemed right. The only thing he could unearth from the depth of his memories is the faint sense of relief and the barely conscious notion, when they entered through the revolving door and took the first breath of the conditioned air, that any place else would be *below their rank*.

The great hall was empty, the concierge stood lonely at the endless wooden reception counter. Amanda was not completely stupid of course, and knew that one night here would blow Detrick's entire yearly budget. And still, she just stood there, and probably waited for a miracle to happen, muttering "please please please" when the reader touched the credit card. And they were on! Ka-ching, funds provided. She committed credit card fraud without a blink of an eye and barely realizing it. The concierge seemed phased out, as Nicolette continuously babbled her mindless speech, directed at him, about rainbows, golden stars, and ponies. He handed them the penthouse keys as if he was a highly developed, human looking robot, and wished them good night in a hoarse tone. They left after a royal breakfast, and they were here in the library right at opening.

What were they thinking? What was *he* thinking? It's his entire fault. He is calling the shots, the girls did not protest against the idea... which is a little strange in itself, that is true.

Detrick was terrified. He felt the weight of responsibility, and the brightly lit room almost physically darkened as he felt a huge, menacing shadow descending over the tiny, bony shoulders of the girl with her back to him, working so diligently. Countering his despair, he felt waves of confidence washing over him, bursting out from his heart, from his chest, from his... tattoo, but it also felt so artificial. He just felt something alien grow inside him, hiding within the strange curves and edges of the symbol on his heart. It was usually like he had a jetpack, or angelic wings pushing him through the day... and yet, in moments of clarity, moments like this, he felt that presence working against his true nature. Maybe this is normal? He never knew what it feels like to have mystical powers, maybe doubts and a new sense of responsibility is normal. He loved it so much, it was like coming home. Like nothing else had happened, just something unlocked his own true potentials! Finally, he could live his life as he always wanted.

Heck, his whole body has changed! He never felt so... powerful, and yet his earthly needs are so distant. Like they were not really needs anymore. Which is also frightening. The constant contrast between pleasure and guilt, empowerment and fear was tearing him apart.

"What will become of us if we go on like this? And what can we do against going insane?"

Maybe he is already dead, with his tattoo taking over his body and the remnants of his soul...

A

Amanda was psyched. She was in super-library-researcher mode. She was studying at least ten books at once, scribbling notes faster than anyone can see while making checks on the internet. She was chasing down the Rundagger-saga like a hound, identifying details, looking for ISDN numbers - without much success. She gathered tiny bits of information, leading to possible clues, but it was like navigating a maze, and after several corners and junctions, she hit a dead end, again and again. She chased a spirit hiding in a myriad mirrors. There was always a glint of hope, a new development, but in the end, the elusive spirit always disappeared behind the next corner - a torn page, a broken URL, a 404 error, a mysterious early death cutting a promising career short at the end of a biography, or a murky spot on the all-important detail of an old photocopy.

It went on like this for hours, when a librarian stepped closer, clearing her throat, not to startle the student buried under a complicated web of research material.

"Excuse me, miss."

Amanda turned towards her with a faint smile. She kept ordering a whole string of books up from the dustiest corners of the library archives, and after a while, the librarians were kind enough to bring the books straight to her, from the drop-off point. So, she was ready to thank them again - but this time, it was someone new. The lady looked ancient, her wrinkles running down on her face being deep like chasms, her grey lips were sharp like blades of knives, and she even wore her hair uptight in a decorative bun, like royalties from the old days. She wore a decent librarian uniform - only a bit older version of it than her colleagues, but an immaculate one nonetheless.

"Oh, well, hello… Mrs. Radzianski" she read her nameplate eloquently "I… didn't have the chance yet…" Amanda felt like, after bombarding the archives with her requests and setting the net connection on fire, now she awakened the ghost of the library itself. She was awed by the presence of this old woman, and her restless, dedicated servitude of the library. It was so impressive.

"No, you did not. I saw your requests popping up in the system, darling. The most intriguing titles, you are looking for on this sunny morning, I must say. Please do excuse me, but I could not stop paying attention." the old lady spoke in an intelligent, reserved and somehow very *noble* tone. Amanda was sure she could listen to her stories for hours on end - if she wasn't so busy.

"Allow me to direct your attention to this old codex of sorts. Quite a rare piece, I might add. I think you would find it interesting. My apologies, if it has nothing to do with your interest, or current research." she put a dusty, thick, old volume on top of some of the books Amanda was already working on, tapping twice on its cover gently, and left before she could properly thank her.

It took her only a glimpse to succumb into it. She encountered the symbol right on the second page. She quickly looked around again, but Mrs. Radzianski already drifted away, to serve other guests with peculiar interests probably. The symbol was not exactly the same, but it was related to what Amanda was looking for, without a doubt.

She progressed through the book furiously. Her reading became almost photographic; she scanned whole pages in mere seconds. She would never have found this book, for neither the author, the publisher; the title (*"Locking Infinity"*) had nothing to do with the findings of her research. She quickly double-checked the reference code of the book in the database, and… she found nothing. Old stamps showed that this book is indeed the property of the city library, yet it was missing from the database. Strange.

The next hours flew away like moments. It was like a big puzzle. It was not a continuation of *Spirits in the Seven Mirrors*, the relation wasn't apparent. But then she slowly got it... it was one big metaphor - the realization urged her to re-read the book she bought as soon as possible. Maybe there is a different way to read that one too... Maybe it is telling something else as well behind the first narrative. She worked through *Locking Infinity*, cross-referencing her notes, checking facts she uncovered on the net, reviewed the old scans, and then she finally got it... it was a code.

The old book contained hidden information which could only get uncovered by people like Amanda, who read the book about the Spirit in the Seven Mirrors, who have been subjected to the power of the Symbol it contains. Amanda realized that there is a Spirit inside them indeed, in five different parts, in five different human beings, each of them carry one part of the symbol of the Spirit... and three of them are together now. Now the old newspaper photocopies about mysterious kidnappings, violent crimes with symbols found on the crime scene, symbols like theirs, but not exactly the same... she felt it starts to make sense now. It is an ancient story, which has been going on for ages, and she is just scraping at the surface.

The Spirit wants all five of the Couriers, the carriers of the Symbols, to assemble. Amanda realized from the metaphors in the book, that two of these Couriers will be drawned together, to become one intimately - this is required for sealing the connection with the Spirit inside. When all five of them are together, with six mirrors around them, the Spirit will be unleashed... taking over them completely.

She turned back to face Detrick. The guy was looking right at her, with a small teardrop glinting on his cheek. They said it aloud together, like one singular thought voiced through two distinct human bodies:

"We need to stop it."

They left hurriedly, after pulling Nicolette from the rows she was wondering inside aimlessly, entertaining herself and the fellow library attendees with amusing little hallucinations.

Mrs. Radzianski followed the three figures staggering out into the bright sunlight, from the vantage point of a ladder attached to the higher shelves, smiling. She knew Amanda stole the old volume, and she knew better than to alert the staff. It was in the best of hands it could be. The afternoon sunlight broke and reflected on the vast old window of the great hall.

If anyone saw her there, they could have easily mistaken the strange golden glow coming from the back of her head, under her silvery white curls, as a playful reflection.

<u>M</u>

Searchlights from the helicopters blazed through the night forest like silver arrows. Michaela took a deep drag from her cigarette as she watched the flames of their campfire. The coppers seemed to overdo it, that fire was giving them away sure enough, yet the choppers were circling around their spot for a good twenty minutes now. She rested her head on Orin's muscular chest, and she felt the greatest safety ever. A SWAT team could storm them any minute, and she could not care less. Let them come, if they will.

Orin caressed her belly gently, than he suddenly moved his arm over her, and grabbed her. He lifted and pulled her over himself as if she was a plastic doll, his big hand ran up to the back of her head and he pushed her face right into his. They joined in a passionate kiss, as the wind brought barks of K-9 units and backing beeps of a truck somewhere, not very far, with the constant echo of the helicopter engines closing in and fading away.

She felt his growing excitement, as she was riding right on top of him. She sheepishly flexed herself up in a riding position and ran her fingers up and down on his well-built breast muscles and ribs, like she was patting a dark horse, getting ready for a long stride. She looked into the black canopy of the whispering trees around them, listening to the mechanical sounds of the armed forces as they prepared the lockdown around them.

She loved teasing Orin, she could not help it. It was a dangerous game, for she could never be sure where she is with him at any given moment. Has he genuinely fallen in love? Does he only want to own her? Does he feel responsible? He did not talk much, though he seemed caring. Caring and increasingly obsessive. She could feel the fires in his eyes even right now, while she is looking away...

"We will see. He will have to wait a little longer... or forever..." she thought to herself mischievously, although as the danger become more and more imminent, with the choppers circling over them, she got turned on by the extremity of the situation. She tries her best to keep him at bay, fighting his strength, and fighting her own willingness at the same time. Who will win? How will all this unfold? All she hoped for is that the outcome will be bloody and fiery. She hated how she ended up, locked up again in the very same box as she found herself all the time before everything... changed. This is so tiresome and futile. Why can't it be normal? Why can't they be like, friends? And maybe something comes out this, when it is time. Why did she have to use her powers on him in the first place? It never was exactly life or death. She did because she could. That is the embarrassing truth. And now she wants him to suffer, just like all the other bastards out there. Michaela caressed the big man below her, swallowing her tears, as the blue and red lights flickered somewhere over the woods. There is no hope, it is just a matter of time now, and all hell will break loose. And even death might not offer peace anymore.

O

"You are surrounded. Lay down, with your face on the ground immediately!"

The trees echoed the loudspeaker. So, they decided to move in, eventually. Orin stood up, slowly. He breathed in the air deeply, as he turned around in a full circle, refusing to lie down, against the hysterical shouts. He hunched himself a bit, like a predator ready to spring at its prey. He was turning around, and then he froze into one direction, his nostrils opening and closing as he breathed vehemently. The wave of testosterone made Michaela's feet feel like clay.

"Keep close to me. Run!" shouted Orin, and charged into the woods. Michaela screamed and dashed right after him. They saw the shadows of the policemen lying in prone positions, raising guns pointed at them from the cover of trunks and standing trees, but Orin seemed to gain speed. Their shouts got to a heightened, panicked cacophony, asking them to stop, than the shots were fired. Orin jumped ahead, like he wanted to hug the incoming bullets, then he crossed his arms in front of him, forming an X with his forearms, and let out a terrifying roar - it sounded like the mountains itself rose from their ancient slumber to avenge the infiltrators who dared to disturb their eon-long slumber. His tattoo covered his arms in a bright purple circular light, and stopped the bullets dead in their tracks, as the nearby squad members emptied their clips into him. He was hit many times, but he merely winced. After the shots were fired, he covered the last few yards like a panther, and jumped over the county police SWAT pickup truck. Michaela did not see anything as she kept running in his tracks, just heard the tore of flesh, the break of bones, gushes of air sweeping out from crushed lungs, and sporadic gunfire, with flashes of bright purple light. She cornered around the trees, wading through the heaps of dry leaves. She heard Orin growling behind her:

"You're doing good baby, you're doing good, we will lose them soon, just keep running…"

The dark figure appeared from nowhere, stepping out from full cover to block her path, raising a handgun. A policeman stepped in front of her, outside the ring of the SWAT commando. He didn't even bother to ask her to stop. Michaela acted instinctively. She launched herself from a tree trunk, up high, covering the remaining distance in a flight, jumped right on the officer with both of her long legs embracing his hip tight, as strong as she could, while her mouth stamped on the lips of the surprised policeman. Her lithe body did not carry enough velocity to knock him to the ground; he just took an awkward step behind and pulled the trigger. And again. The two shots sent two tremors up her small body, as she sucked hard on the lip of the officer and her charm overcame him. He kneeled down, holding her in his arms, with tears running down his young, handsome face, looking at the girl in utter disbelief. Michaela smiled at him, sadly, while she coughed up a little blood.

"So… sorry…" gasped the policeman under her. These were his last words, as Orin got around him, and broke his neck with grabbing his head in both hands, and jerked it around. He grabbed Michaela under his armpit like a bag of bread, and ran out from the trees, to the Woodside parking lot.

He threw her down on the tarmac with great strength, yet with great compassion, lessening the impact and laying her down gently in the end.

"Babe… stay with me, you hear me? Where does it hurt?" he asked in a hushed tone. He gently rubbed the blood on her belly, to look for the entry wound.

"I… I can't feel…"

"I know baby, just stay with me it will all be alright! Where is that freaking wound…?"

"Orin… I… God, I don't feel pain. It doesn't hurt. Anymore." Michaela spat some blackish blood on the tarmac with a giggle.

"WHA…" said the big tight end, losing his patience and turning her around aggressively. He checked her back - there was some blood on her back as well, but no sign of an exit wound. She seemed unharmed!

"You can't lose me so easily, big man.," said Michaela, biting on her tongue, and jumping on the passenger seat of the Mustang. "Now where the hell are my cigarettes?"

Half an hour, and several cigarettes later, they were cruising along the road getting closer to the city.

"Okay." Orin broke a long silence. "It was quite fun. Yeah..."

"It was awesome." added Michaela, nodding affirmatively.

"...but if we go on like this, they will bring tanks. And jets. Hell, they will even nuke us eventually."

"Wow. I've never been nuked before."

"You know it is fun, like, that we can't die. But, you know, I mean, I'm sure we can die eventually. We don't know the limits, how this works."

"Like, by getting nuked?"

"Yeah baby, that is kinda rough. Ever saw those photos from Hiroshima? People actually burned into the walls like *shadows*, you get that? How can you heal from *that*?"

"I don't wanna end up like a shadow on the wall. How boring that sounds!"

"Yeah, so, you know, thing is, Abrams tanks and Hellfire rockets are doing a pretty decent job at blowing stuff to pieces. Like, into molecules."

"I dunno. I don't play video games."

"Yeah. Exactly! That's what I'm saying. We can't play, like, GTA 6 Ultra-Undead version forever. They could capture us alive. Wash our brains. Or exorcise the crap out of us! You know this thing we got..." said Orin, raising his tattooed forehand from the steering for a second "... this is not something Mother Nature can produce. I'm... quite sure of that."

"Okay Orin. You got a plan? What you wanna do? Maybe we should go to Switzerland. Can you snowboard?"

"Nah. Sounds fun though. Never been to Europe. Kinda hard to get on a plane with an APB out on you though. Any ideas how to get there?"

"Stop."

"Wha?"

"I said STOP! Turn around RIGHT NOW, darn it!" Michaela shouted and banged the glove compartment with her high heel to add some extra weight to her request.

"Wow. Okay miss." Orin stepped on the gas, steered the car over to the left lane, than slightly back towards the right, and then turned the wheel hard to the left again, with his right hand jerking up the handbrake.

The Mustang roared and drifted around, with its tires burning, throwing blue smoke all over the road. Michaela held her head high and pushed it back into the headrest while Orin was neighing like the wild horses their ride got its name from.

"Don't drive recklessly unless you can't die, kids!" shouted Orin into the night, and he floored it, when the nose of the car pointed to the opposite direction, right where they came from.

"So, Switzerland that way? Any plan on crossing the Atlantic?" he asked with a big smile.

"You can drop that RPM back. I just want to check that billboard out."

Orin slowed the car down and turned its nose to their left, driving slightly off the tarmac. The headlights fell on a great billboard they passed earlier, a few seconds and a spectacular donut ago.

"See that?" asked Michaela, and lit a cigarette, to look more investigative. There wasn't a single sound out here in the night, but the chirping of crickets over the low murmur of the V8 in idle power. The billboard showed a pop art poster with a slight gothic feel, telling all who passes this road that a traveling theme park is finally arrived into the city - incredible fun and otherworldly magic awaits everyone who dares to enter.

"Yeah. Geez. That logo looks pretty much like our tats."

"Yeee-aaah. A little too much, even. So, I suggest that, before hitting Switzerland, we go and check out the Wondrous Wonderbilt for ourselves."

<u>N</u>

The streetlights cast their rays inside the car, one by one, as they passed under them. Nicolette looked at the moving lights reflecting from the large golden medal hanging from one of the necklaces she got from her worshippers. She played with locking the tiny rays of reflections in place, and slowly molding them into the symbol she wore on her face. She captured one tiny reflection from almost each lamp they zoomed past, and listened to the front seat conversation half-heartedly. Detrick and Amanda, while she was happy to have them around, since they both carried the symbol, took things way too seriously. Ever since they left the library, and hit a drive thru, they can't stop talking about stuff Amanda uncovered in an ancient book.

"We need to find the other two." "All five of us are needed to use the Code." They even mentioned something awkward about the importance of "not having sex," because that would "seal" the connection they have and bring the Spirit closer to its goal. Do they talk about the One she is serving? Well, what else would somebody, wearing its sign on one's own body even want, than to serve its goals? Nicolette did not care much about sexy time anymore; she had a much deeper relationship with the One, way beyond bodily pleasures. It is locked in its place, inside her, and will never go away. They even considered something about leaving the country, all of them, into each different country? To surely never meet? Why would somebody do that? Besides, they spoke about unifying and figuring out together how to use that Code together. Gosh. These guys really need to give themselves a break!

"Heeeeeeyyyy, Miss Nerdy queen, Mister Knight-in-shiny-armor, why don't you take a little chill pill and listen to ol' Nicolette for a second, not being so all-important for a moment?" she broke their conversation and edged herself between the two sporty front seats of the Celica, pushing the medal ahead so the others can see the 3D light symbol she crafted meticulously.

"Nicolette, darling, why don't you put that light-thingie away a bit, so other people can't see clearly that we do magic, would you, please?" asked Amanda in a kind, warm voice, like she was talking to a four year old. "...and you up there, WOULD YOU TURN TO GREEN ALREADY." she added, losing her temper about the longish wait the traffic light forced on them. A light screech of tires was heard, and some grumbled swears, as a car coming to cross the junction from the left stopped abruptly. The light above them immediately turned to yellow and then green, within a split second.

"....whoopsie... I'm sorry, didn't mean to interrupt..." sang Amanda sheepishly and quickly navigated her car through the junction.

"I know what you guys need. A little fun at a THEME PARK!" said Nicolette, and held a flyer between the front seats. "I found this at the library while looking around trying not to get bored out of my mind. They just arrived in town!"

Amanda stopped the car with stepping on the brakes, and flipped on the emergency blinker with a mental command. They looked at the whirling symbol at the center of flyer, which promised an unforgettable evening for everyone who comes to visit the Wondrous Wonderbilt.

8

DAMON

Special Agent Lisa Moss leaned forward on the leather sofa in the spacious entry hall of the Old Oak Hotel. Officer Fitzpatrick came to rejoin her and her companion, who sat laid back in the shade. The sheriff had a troubled look on his face.

"Let me guess. Security cameras either did not record anything or it's all blurry. And they could not come up with a decent description." she said with a grin.

"Well, it depends whether you deem the following as decent enough:" he answered, clearing his throat, and raising his tiny notebook up a bit. 'A blonde prince, a beautiful angel radiating heavenly light, and a little girl in grey robes'

Moss burst another gum bubble. "Well. Sounds definitely fitting."

"Fitting… just… what do you mean?"

"The King, the Priestess, and the Wizard." - said a rasping voice from the shade covering the sofa. He leaned into the light as he lit a cigarette. "In this case, a wizar-dette." He was a charismatic man, wearing a white shirt with no tie, his silver hair combed back on his head, sporting silver stubble. Despite the lack of pigmentation, Fitzpatrick guessed he is at the end of his forties. Handsome or not, good mannered or not - the sheriff started to lose his temper, faster, rather than slower. Blood has been spilled, good men lost, or facing prosecution, and the tides of chaos seem to reach higher and higher every day. He is fed up with riddles.

"Sir, apart from your mysterious phone call mentioning the involvement of the supernatural, and flashing a CIA badge when questioned earlier, may I ask what exactly do you base your most interesting assumptions upon?"

The man smiled and blew some smoke. After a long pause, he held his cigarette in his mouth, and unbuttoned the left cuff of his shirt. Slowly and thoroughly, he curled the sleeve of his shirt up, until his arm was free, up until the elbow. Then he turned his hand to reveal the tattoo on his inner arm. Fitzpatrick turned several shades paler. His tattoo looked very much like all the others, like the ones Campbell and Kaminski got made, similar to the huge image the astray Jennings girl painted on the wall of her room. One difference was that the symbol on his arm had a very intricate outer frame, like the complex image was surrounded with an even more complex pattern.

Moss burst another bubble and intervened.

"Okay. Fitzpatrick. I know…no, I have a pretty strong guess about how you feel about being dragged into the city to investigate a credit card fraud, when there are psychos out there, running rampant somewhere in the county. I need to make it clear, that these cases are related. Closely. Why don't you sit down please? It's time I bring you up to speed."

"Preciate it, Agent Moss."

"Okay. So. I'm far from putting together the full picture yet, you see, and we don't have the time to fill you in with all the tiny details, and all the…" her gaze wandered over to the man at the other side of the table "…*historical* implications of this case, let alone tapping into the field of the possible explanations. We are sticking to the facts. However, facts are… kinda flimsy, in this case. So let me explain this the quickest way possible. Okay?"

Fitzpatrick nodded. His mouth was very much cat fishy again, and he looked lost. He looked like someone who could really use a nice big glass of jam and a bucket of donuts right now.

"Okay. Now let me ask you this. Do you know the TV show about Buffy?"

"WHAT? The high school vampire slayer? Holy hell. Sure, I do. Why?"

"Officer Fitzpatrick, for the sake of closing this investigation successfully, and knowing that we have now arrived to a point where we can safely assume that we are facing a significant threat to national security, I would kindly ask you to, from this point onwards, until a yet undisclosed point in time, please do not consider the contents of the aforementioned TV show as a television drama, but rather, as a sort of documentary, based on real life events."

A

"Fifteen minutes, Director Rundagger."

"Thank you, Marla."

The director bound his tie, watching himself in his mirror, while whistling a merry tune.

"Director?"

"Yes, Marla?"

"I... I know it might sound silly... but I... can't wait for the show tonight. Somehow I'm convinced - this night will be special!" said the young assistant with a slightly trembling voice.

The director smiled and nodded to her. "I feel that too, Marla. In fact, I'm also, as you put it, *convinced*, that this night will be memorable." The assistant smiled to the mirror image of the director and held her tiny fists upwards in excitement, then quickly left.

"Oh, yes, darling. You have no idea. This night will be the start of a whole new chapter in our history." - whispered the director to himself, as he carefully raised his golden pendant, which was shaped in an extremely intricate nonfigurative shape, with many curves and edges, and took it on.

M

Nicolette threw her huge paper bag of popcorn up in the air, and jumped in the center of the dancing area of the stage, exploding in a rainbow of light. The crowd let out sounds of surprise and then cheered for the new show element in deafening uproar. Amanda hid behind her laptop screen, but her fingers moved so quickly on the keyboard that they become blurred. She worked the speaker systems, directed some powerful spotlights on Nicolette, to make her glittering even more spectacular, and took over the sound control system, starting a song he found in the database and she felt as a fitting one. She giggled evilly as she saw with half her eye that the DJ up in his dark little command center threw his hands up in the air in desperation, as the controls seemed to come to life and do whatever they wanted, and he threw his headphone to the ground.

Detrick grabbed the microphone in the center - the ceremony master said it was open mike at this part of the show anyway! - And although he never thought of himself as a performer, he stepped in right when the vocals started in the next song Amanda launched.

> *We're caught in a trap*
> *I can't walk out*
> *Because I love you too much baby*

The crowds screamed as Detrick left the best Elvis imitators in shame; even his moves were fully authentic. The audience ran to the dance floor still occupied by the professional dancers in flocks, shouting in ecstasy.

> *Why can't you see?*
> *What you're doing to me*
> *When you don't believe a word I say?*

A circle of people danced and clapped around Nicolette, who showered them in the most amazing seventies light show in the history of entertainment, all the while enhancing their joy and utter happiness. She would shoot huge rays of light towards the disco balls, at the most dramatic high points of the song.

> *We can't go on together*
> *With suspicious minds (suspicious minds)*
> *And we can't build our dreams*
> *On suspicious minds*

The crowds went wild as a hulking dark figure took his lithe girlfriend and literally *threw* her up into the dome of the Wondrous Wonderbilts Main Hall, in an incredible feat of strength and precision. The girl grabbed a hanging pole there, and started performing a pole dance, which was equally graceful and arousing, gathering male attention rapidly. A symbol on her chest glisten bright purple light, a symbol, which seemed to be a smaller portion of the Wonderbilts elaborate logo.

> *So, if an old friend I know*
> *Stops by to say hello*
> *Would I still see suspicion in your eyes?*

Amanda quickly spotted her and directed some lights over her so her moves became the center of the show. "Gotcha." she nodded for herself. "Looks like we got the last two Couriers."

> *Here we go again*
> *Asking where I've been*
> *You can't see these tears are real*
> *I'm crying (Yes I'm crying)*

Security and technicians ran around like headless chickens - they were in no easy situation as Amanda fed a continuously changing distortion effect back into the main radio line, so there were a few seconds when it sounded normal, but it always fell apart after a while, just to stabilize again. The staff could not decide whether to try to communicate electronically, or leave it and try to manage to control the situation without it. Amanda gazed up to the VIP box. A tall, elegant figure stood there with a huge golden pendant, and a hysterical assistant was trying to tell him something, shouting over the loudness of the show, pulling her headset away from her ears. The tall figure just stood there, unfazed. He maybe even smiled, Amanda realized, when crosschecking with the security camera feed. "Well, Mister. If you run this show, you can rest assured. It is in the best hands now." she said to herself, and programmed another fabulous barrage of laser effects onto the stage.

We can't go on together
With suspicious minds (suspicious minds)
And we can't build our dreams
On suspicious minds

O

Hours later, the five tattooed strangers staggered through the improvised streets between the converted trucks and great tents of the Wondrous Wonderbilt. They were still high on adrenaline, dopamine, and every possible chemical the human body creates when it feels really good. Their mood skyrocketed up and stayed there. Nothing seemed to matter on this beautiful evening. Nicolette walked before them, dancing, throwing balls of light around them and all over the guests who decided to visit the traveling theme park tonight. No one seemed to be scared or repulsed by the huge, glowing tattoo on her face, neither by the similar tattoos on different parts of the bodies on the four youngsters walking behind her, hand in hand.

"Mirror Maze! Woohoo!" screamed Nicolette, and dashed right in. No matter where they have found themselves within the theme park, whether they were shooting targets, had a go at the hammering machine (at which Orin hit the jackpot of course), everyone welcomed them cheerfully, every service was offered to them free of charge, their pockets were filled with freebie candy and lollipop. The bars in front of the Mirror Maze also miraculously opened up, letting the screaming Nicolette dive right in.

"Yes, my friends, now the time finally comes!" a loud voice rumbled - the way it sounded, it came straight out of the sky. "The moment you've ALL been waiting for! Who dares to enter the Mirror Maze, and uncover the secret hiding in the Chamber of the Seven Mirrors?"

Amanda froze, like she was struck with lightning. She felt the speakers around them, on the poles, as they were throbbing with the high volume of the mysterious voice. But she knew it, felt it, that the voice came not only from the outside - it rang, somehow, within her head as well.

"Det... Detrick! Something... something is not right!"

She wanted to go inside with all her heart. She wanted to go in so bad, that she got scared. Her tattoo seemed to come to life, swelled into a big purple bulge on her arm, pulling her inside.

"What's the matter, babe? Amanda?" Detrick was standing in front of her, his eyes being distant, like instead of looking at her, he was looking far into a hidden horizon. "Don't you feel all right? This night is... amazing. I'm so glad we are here, together, with you."

"Detrick, please, listen to me, there was... there was something we came here for, remember? Something... important..." Amanda touched the side of her head, as it ached from the strain of trying to remember, while waves of ecstasy and rejoice washed over her from the wonders she experienced in the last few hours. "You... please... stop them!" she shouted at Detrick, with a tear trembling in her eye, pointing toward the sparkling tent of the Mirror Maze. She watched in horror as Orin and Michaela, hand in hand, went inside the tent, following Nicolette, whose amused shouts and laughter echoed out from the corridors. Before they disappeared in the doorway, Michaela turned halfway back and threw a wicked smile at the shivering girl.

"Come on in, sweetheart. Don't fight the inevitable." Amanda collapsed.

"Amanda, please, I'm here for you, okay? What's the matter? We came to find these guys, remember? They have the tattoos! We are all five now, together, we will figure it all out, everything will be fine from here! Let's just enjoy this one night together, have fun! We will work everything out tomorrow." hushed Detrick, and lead the sobbing Amanda inside.

<u>N</u>

The Mirror Maze had all kinds of mirrors on its walls. Ones where you looked tall, short, fat, thin, distorted, disfigured, happy, sad, high in Heaven, deep down in Hell, flying high with the angels, or torn apart in the abyss by devils.

The insane screams and laughter of Nicolette lead them like an echo. The Maze wasn't big at all, only a few corridors, with some cheap visual tricks made the intersections more challenging. Yet, after a while, they could not tell if they were inside for minutes, or hours have passed. Their tattoos blazed in the dim light, the reflections coming over them everywhere. The symbol appeared at the most unrecognizable places, sometimes enlarged into huge shapes that seemed to devour them, sometimes splintered into myriad tiny bits, like a galaxy that they become the center of.

"Mirrors, they are everywhere…" breathed Amanda while she gripped the arm of Detrick as hard as she could. "We… we should not be around so many mirrors, Detrick…" she uttered, but she feared losing the others more than anything, so she held on.

A long scream marked that Nicolette has probably found the central room.

"I'm here, I'm here, I'm all yours, finally, I'm all yo-ho-ho-ho-ho-urs" she screamed and burst into a loud crying. "It is so beautiful, oh my, this is it, finally…"

Amanda turned around the corner with Detrick. The last room, in the center, was rectangular, one single box shaped space, although it was hard to tell - the floor, the ceiling, and every wall was fully reflective, multiplying the five guests up into infinity. Nicolette sat in the center collapsed, overwhelmed by the beauty of the millions of reflections of her symbol, dancing around her.

"Yes, Chosen Ones, now you can uncover the secret of the Seven Mirrors! Just form a circle, facing outward, and see the wonder!"

The loud, deep voice followed them even here, probably coming from hidden speakers, maybe from right inside their heads - they could not tell the difference, neither did they care.

Amanda's tattoo was practically throbbing. She had every desire to follow the instructions of the strange, deep voice, and she was equally terrified to death about the consequences.

"This is only six, right? Six mirrors." wondered Orin. "Where is the seventh?"

He and Michaela stood by Nicolette, who slowly rose to her feet, trembling from emotions. They were turning their heads around in awe. When they looked back at the final two arriving, their eyes were also shining with the same purple glow, as their tattoos - or so it seemed to Amanda.

"Guys…" she started, slowly, while they joined the other three at the center.

"I know this… might… sound a bit awkward and… certainly… incredibly… out of place, but… did you… have you… happened to… so… uhm. Did you sleep together, the two of you, lately? Or like, ever?"

"HOLD YOUR HANDS and face the mirrors! See the amazing truth!" - barked the voice.

Orin and Michaela looked at Amanda like she fell straight from the Moon, right that second.

"What... what do you mean, you want like... you wanna do it like *here*, in front of these mirrors?" asked Orin, and laughed at the geeky girl in amazement and disbelief.

Michaela smiled.

"Yeah, actually. He screw me like an animal last night, out in the swamps, on the hood of our stolen Mustang, sweetie. Is that exactly what you wanted to know?"

"HOLD HANDS AND LOOK INTO THE MIRRORS!" the voice commanded, and they all were shaken by its power, and quickly stood the form a circle, and reached for each other's hands.

Amanda coughed and dropped to half her knee. Detrick quickly reached after her, to help her up, but she grabbed her own arm, her tattooed arm, and held it down back, like she was fighting one hand with the other.

"The seventh mirror... the seventh mirror...Detrick...HELP!" she screamed.

"What is wrong with you, Amanda? Tell me, I'm here, I don't know, I don't understand..." said Detrick, who held Amanda's right arm. He felt the familiar cold shiver running up his spine, his heart below his swollen tattoo beat so hard it almost exploded. Something wasn't right... but what? He knew he should remember, there was something important Amanda found out in the library, he just could not clear his head with all the emotions raging inside him. He felt like he was straddled in a car that was speeding towards the chasm... but what should he do?

Michaela touched the back of Amanda, her tattoo in full glow, and whispered:

"C'mon, honey, just let it go and hold my hand. You will enjoy it. I promise."

"What is happening, what is happening, why don't you stand up already, oh my god, I want this so bad, please, STAND UP ALREADY!" they all, except Nicolette, covered their ears for the second, as the girl with the tattooed face began to lose it, and her voice, in the excitement, got amplified by her powers, in the small, mirrored room.

"HOLD HANDS AND FACE THE... JUST what do you think you are doing in this room?" - asked the voice, with genuine surprise.

"Oh no, oh no, oh no...! PLEASE make this happen now, I can't bear it anymore! I want to be FREE!" screamed Nicolette in agony, and her emotions started to shake her body like it was a single leaf caught up in a winter storm.

Amanda was almost standing again, while holding her tattooed arm, pushing it into her own stomach "The seventh... will appear... in the center...." she gasped "And the Spirit... will be free..."

"This is OFF LIMITS to visitors, get away from... HOLD HANDS AND FACE THE..." the voice commanded them, but it sounded like it was busy with talking to someone else as well.

"FACE THE MIR..." a loud bang was heard, and the sound fell silent.

"NO!" screamed Nicolette, and started breathing heavily, overcome by a panic attack - she wanted to tear herself apart to release the being inside her, rattling her body like a caged beast.

"...roars" Amanda ended the last word of the voice, finally giving in, and reaching to the hand of Michaela on her left. But she never got to touch it.

Nicolette's scream reached a new height. She mustered all her strength into her frustration, visions from her last few days haunted her, the sickly bodies in the alley, the tears of her sister, the unearthly pain of the tattoo needle working her eyes, and the loud bang that ended the voice which was guiding her towards infinite freedom. She unleashed all her power in one single scream.

The massive electromagnetic burst knocked all of them unconscious, except her, and exploded all the mirrors of the Mirror Maze around her into tiny splinters.

By the time the medics arrived to the scene, she peeled most of the skin off her own face, with the glass splinters, crying bloody tears, mixed in with the black ink of her destroyed symbol.

EPILOGUE

Amanda lay in a hospital bed. Everything was white and peaceful. She changed the channels of the television screen hanging in the corner, by the blinks of her eye. She glanced over to Detrick's bed, and turned down the volume a bit more, to let him sleep. Her head was still fuzzy, like it was turned to a dead channel.

A man came inside. Grey hair, but still handsome. Immaculate, white shirt, with the sleeves turned up. Amanda saw that he had a tattoo on his inner arm, just like she did. It looked exactly the same - the elaborate symbol, but now, she realized, was encircled, with another intricate pattern. Looking down on her own arm, she almost fainted: hers looked the same now. Someone added a complex pattern around her own tattoo while she was unconscious.

"Who are you?" she asked. The man smiled for a while before he answered.

"We will have plenty of time to properly get to know each other. For now, let's just say, you and I, well... we will understand each other well."

Amanda glanced over to Detrick.

"Will he be all right?" she asked, afraid of what the answer might hold.

"Yes! Certainly. I just wanted to grab the opportunity to speak with you alone."

"Did we... stop it?"

"Yes, you did. In fact, you *yourself* did. You held out long enough to stop the spirit from breaking through."

"What happened with... the others?"

"Orin came to first. Such a strong guy. A true Warrior, he definitely is. He grabbed Michaela and ran for it. Unfortunately."

"And... Nick?"

The man sighed and looked out the window for a while. Then he suddenly continued, like, he decided there is no reason to hold back anything now.

"The medics, who got to her are... still in ER, with third degree burns. She blasted them when they approached to assist her. Then, she left."

"Left? Just, like... left?"

"Yes. You won't see her anytime soon. Hopefully."

Amanda let that sink in. She wanted to save her so much. She deserved it. She took a deep breath.

"So, when can we leave? Go home?"

"Oh, you're leaving tomorrow. You are only under observation through the coming night, there will be some routine checks in the morning, and then you will probably be on your way. However..." he added with a faint smile, pulling out an envelope from his chest pocket "...you will have a little something to take care of, after leaving this place. Alas, I must bid adieux! I will see you very soon. It was a real pleasure, Amanda," said the strange figure, and left, like he was from a dream.

Only the lengthy envelope reminded her of his presence. Amanda opened it, and her lips fell open as she realized the contents. Two airplane tickets.

"What the... don't tell me we're flying..." she mumbled, and turned the ticket with her name on it, to see the destination.

"...to Switzerland?"